PENGUIN BOOKS

FABLES OF THE IRISH INTELLIGENTSIA

Nina FitzPatrick is of Polish-Irish ancestry. She travels widely and wildly in Europe and is currently working on a novel based on her own misadventures.

FABLES
Of The
Irish Intelligentsia

NINA FITZPATRICK

PENGUIN BOOKS

PENGUIN BOOKS
Published by the Penguin Group
Viking Penguin, a division of Penguin Books USA Inc.,
375 Hudson Street, New York, New York 10014, U.S.A.
Penguin Books Ltd, 27 Wrights Lane, London W8 5TZ, England
Penguin Books Australia Ltd, Ringwood, Victoria, Australia
Penguin Books Canada Ltd, 10 Alcorn Avenue, Suite 300,
Toronto, Ontario, Canada M4V 3B2
Penguin Books (N.Z.) Ltd, 182–190 Wairau Road,
Auckland 10, New Zealand

Penguin Books Ltd, Registered Offices:
Harmondsworth, Middlesex, England

First published in Great Britain
by Fourth Estate Limited 1991
Published in Penguin Books 1993

1 3 5 7 9 10 8 6 4 2

Publisher's Note:
These are works of fiction. Names, characters, places, and incidents either are the product of the author's imagination or are used fictitiously, and any resemblance to actual persons, living or dead, events, or locales is entirely coincidental.

LIBRARY OF CONGRESS CATALOGING IN PUBLICATION DATA
FitzPatrick, Nina.
Fables of the Irish intelligentsia/Nina FitzPatrick.
p.   cm.
ISBN 0 14 01.7324 2
1. Fables, English—Irish authors.   2. Ireland—Fiction.
I. Title.
PR6056.I89F33   1993
823'.914—dc20   92–31703

Printed in the United States of America

For Tone and Ulf, as promised

Contents

Prologue

There is a valley in Ireland called Glenn Bolcain. It has four gaps to the wind, a breezy bay, bogs to the north, blue hills to the south, larks in the air and healing herbs in every cleft and cranny. Each year the madmen of Ireland congregate there to drink from the holy well and eat watercress and young nettles. They rush to the valley of their own accord without guidance or help from anybody.

Those who come to Glenn Bolcain are filled with loathing for places familiar to them and with a desire for places unknown. There they mingle with their own kind and leap and fly without let or hindrance. When not agitated either horizontally or vertically they sit around and tell one another lies. At night they roost in the trees like rooks in a rookery.

Now and then a squabble breaks out among them over who has the right to lodge in Glenn Bolcain. For where lies the boundary between lunacy and reason?

Only the farmers seem to know and they bolt their windows and doors for fear of the edgemen.

It is said that madmen visit Glenn Bolcain to heal themselves. This is not true. They don't want to be healed at all. The come there to relish the frenzies only that valley can feed.

A Free Man

I'd better tell the story quickly before it all happens to myself.

Bernard Slattery was a professor of Sanskrit and a father of four. When I met him at the staff party he looked as prim and spry as a merganser. Mergansers have this quiff of hair on the head, a quick side to side flick of the beak and a knack of making a brisk exit underwater. Slattery appeared and disappeared at different ends of the Common Room in search of prey. Finally he popped up beside me and snatched at the loose button on my jacket. I can't recall just now what we talked about. But it must have been either Hindu influences on Neoplatonism, salary differentials, or the way our Academic Council pisses on the Humanities. Slattery was as boring as tripe in oil.

I thought of him as the archetypal family man. For him love began at home and that was the problem. His wife Rita was an unemployed professional actress. She had developed huge muscles and a foul tongue while rehearsing the *Non Stop Connolly Show*. After a glass of

wine she would shed curses like goat's marbles. Bernard
would shake and go ha ha ha.

Slattery had a secret ambition to be the Dean of Arts.
But he blew it by writing incomprehensible articles on
Cosmic Consciousness. I disliked the cock of the walk
side of him but felt drawn to the seeker on the Path.
Which is why we occasionally had a few jars together. At
the end of our chat about Hinduism or the decline of the
Humanities he would invariably say, 'Malachi, you must
come home for dinner sometimes.'

And I would reply, 'Of course, Bernard, I'd love to.'

But I knew his wife would never allow it because I had
a bad influence on people.

I hadn't seen him for at least six months when the
letter arrived. It was very intimate, which alarmed me.
He was lecturing on the virtues of tar water in Bishop
Berkeley at the Berkeley Summer School in Wexford.
There he had this supersensory, Neoplatonic experi-
ence. He was in a state of bliss. Only I would understand.
Could I come straight away?

I didn't want to drive to bloody Wexford. But then it
occurred to me that by going there I could kill two birds
with one stone. *Plegadis falcinellus*, a glossy ibis, was
reported feeding on the slobs. Half the bird watchers in
the country had been to spy it out. And then there was
Slattery, the mystic merganser. So off I went.

When I got to Wexford there was no sign of Bernard
Slattery. There were restrained rumours. He had flipped
his lid, hit the bottle, gone to Ballybunion with a PAP.
And all these blessings had befallen him within the space
of three days.

I envied him through a long night of Carlsbergs. Next

day I drove home, sick as a parrot. I forgot all about the glossy ibis. I spent three days in bed drying out. I exaggerate. It wasn't three days.

His next letter was apologetic. He couldn't meet me in Wexford because his Polish American Princess wanted to dance her T'ai Chi on the Hill of Uisneach. He went on to explain how he had met her. He had first seen her at the Summer School reception. She was wearing a pink Fiorucci sweat shirt and Banana Republic khaki shorts. During the party he had gone up to his room and found the air impregnated with her scent. This was a revelation. He went downstairs, kissed her before everybody and brought her back to his room.

During the night she told him that he was the last of the true humanists and that she herself had been George Russell in a previous incarnation. It never happened like this before. Their six bodies had embraced, that is, the atmic, buddhic, causal, mental, astral and physical. Leaving his wife and four children would not be a sacrifice but a necessity. Could I put him up for a few nights?

I couldn't. But I could offer him advice. I wrote him a long letter with lots of instructions. He should avoid:

(a) priests, especially those who were trendy or friends of the family;
(b) interviews with marriage counsellors;
(c) going on the batter.

He should turn a deaf ear to gibes about:

(a) the mid-life crisis;
(b) the male menopause;
(c) endogenous depression;

(d) living in mortal sin.

Above all he should avoid psychiatrists. I threw in a few abusive words about his wife to give him heart for the enterprise. It was a man's letter to a man. It spoke the language of the tribe.

Slattery never got it. His wife intercepted it. More than that, she passed it round among the Faculty wives. They said I should be hung.

When he returned to our town he was a new man. I came across him in a pub eating chowder and singing his own Sanskrit version of 'Galway Bay'. Now and then he would stop and shout, 'Fuck the begrudgers and the technocrats, ha ha ha!'

His shirt was open, the silk polka-dot tie hung around his neck like a stole and he no longer stank of Brut. He was buying drinks for everyone.

We all drew secret pleasure from watching this transformation. He ordered me to phone the Church of Ireland rector because he wished to convert to Protestantism. Like myself he was a deeply religious man and wouldn't dream of marrying outside the Church. The pub was full of unemployed atheists and agnostics who decried this move, but I supported him. He told me, on the quiet, that he had rented a large house for himself and the PAP. He had filled the fridge with Norwegian elk and Hungarian Tokay. His girl was due in a week's time.

While Bernard spent happy days and nights in pubs arguing for the recovery of Spirit and the re-sacralisation of nature, his wife got up on her bike. She set up a network of priests, psychologists, academics, Gardai, general practitioners and out-of-work actors.

Poor Bernard was sick. Not for the first time. He needed Tender Loving Care, the poor fucker. He was a sick man. The last time he went round the twist it was just the same. He booked himself into a hotel in Portugal as the Lord Mervue and Renmore. He ran up a big huge bill on international telephone calls. They had to bring him home. It took thirty wallops of ECT to straighten the cunt out. This time he had got through £1,500 in two weeks. The elative phase would be followed by massive depression. That's what nobody understood. Word of God, the sooner he was caught the better.

Some days later when I was sitting on the floor of my office trying to meditate, Bernard rang. He was very agitated.

'The Catholic mafia are after me. Come to The Fallen Gentry and Other Souls immediately.'

I cancelled my lectures and went to The Fallen Gentry. There he was drinking his favourite Tokay.

'*Vinum regnum Rex Vinorum*!' he shouted as I entered.

'Professor Slattery has just been visited by his wife's brother, the family doctor and the College chaplain,' whispered the barman. 'He threw them all out!'

'Here's to life, love and lust!' cried Bernard. He was as boastful as a blue jay.

In the restaurant upstairs he expounded the primacy of consciousness, the imminence of the Apocalypse and the reality of vibrations on the subtle planes. He no longer wanted to join the Church of Ireland. Instead he was planning to go with his girl to the New Age Commune in Findhorn.

'In that case you'd better watch your money,' I said, guiltily finishing off a lobster in brandy.

'Not at all!' he shouted. 'You see, the Father, God bless him, won't last another year. And he's rotten with money. And there's an aunt as well, ha ha ha! Eighty–five years of age and a large . . . '

He half rose from the table.

'Get that charlatan out of here! You Judas, you traitor!' he roared.

Not at me. At Dr MacAdoo who stood in the doorway like a Master of Hounds. MacAdoo's face was red with magisterial anger, Slattery's was white with offended dignity. He kept ordering the waitress to throw MacAdoo out on his f-u-c-k-i-n-g ear.

MacAdoo beckoned me over. He waved a piece of paper in my face.

'Your friend can either come quietly or we'll take him by force. He's been committed.'

I looked out of the window. Three guards were grouped at the opposite corner. The hounds were closing in. I felt like an ulan at the Charge of Samosierra.

'I'll see what I can do,' I told the doctor.

Slattery's choice was between voluntary insanity and compulsory insanity. I advised him to choose the first. That way he would be free to leave the madhouse when the air cleared a bit. So we went to the Psychiatric Unit and checked him in. Slattery took it bravely. He insisted on my sending him copies of all his recent publications to distribute to the patients. Next day he discovered that he had been committed as insane for wasting family property and psychopathic behaviour. On his wife's insistence he was forbidden all visitors, including the PAP.

Commedia finita est, I thought to myself. Another good man gone. But I was wrong.

Later that evening I was sitting in my office with Sven Jakobson and Luke Kelly. Luke and myself were drinking whiskey. (I keep two naggins for emergencies under my desk in a pair of kangaroo boots: Powers in the left, Paddy in the right.) Sven, as usual, sipped his own supply of 0.5% Lett Ø1 which he had brought over from Sweden. They knew all about Slattery. Luke was very depressed. Sven, on the other hand, sat there delighted, shaking his head and repeating, '*Utroligt, utroligt.*' For Sven, Galway was always *utroligt* or *vidunderligt*. The only brush with the transcendent he had in his own life was once being plunged in darkness on the Stockholm underground when the electricity failed.

We were leafing through Slattery's offprints and nodding our heads in judicious melancholy. I was just about to deliver an *In memoriam* speech when the door was flung open and whom did we see?

Slattery in his pyjamas and slippers.

'How the hell did you get here?' I asked.

'I ran. I can run when I want to. Get me a lawyer.'

We locked the door and got on the phone.

The lawyer was a callous pelican whose goitre trembled while he swallowed all the evenements. Five minutes later the hospital attendants arrived. They pounded on the door while Slattery made his statement. The pelican couldn't be of much help. Slattery was trapped by the terms of the Mental Health Act of 1947 or whenever it was.

In desperation we rang the chief psychiatrist at the hospital and made a deal. Slattery would once more be surrendered to his care but on four conditions. *Primo*: that his girl would be allowed to visit him. *Secundo*: that

Sven, Luke and myself would be allowed to see him on alternate days. *Tercio*: that he would have access to his lawyer. *Quarto*: that he would be allowed to distribute his manifesto 'Trolls and Humanists' to the hospital staff.

Before leaving, Bernard slipped me the key to his rented house. He had managed to conceal it from everybody.

That night, when the pubs closed, Sven, Luke and myself went to the house of destiny. Like hungry scald crows we threw ourselves on the elk. But even the Tokay couldn't raise our dead spirits. I remember accusing Sven of being a prosaic Lutheran who understood nothing. He kept looking at himself and chanting his mantra: 'I'm lonely. Lonely. *Ensom*. Yes.'

Luke sat in the drawing room with the light off, crying.

When my turn came to visit Slattery I found him playing scrabble with a manic jogger. The jogger had been running forty-five miles a day before they got him. He was skin and bone. Slattery, by contrast, looked as pale and plump as a broiler chicken. Both were drugged to their eyeballs with Paxil.

Slattery told me what a lovely man the psychiatrist was. The air of the room had a faint fetid smell. It must have been the drugs evaporating off their skin. The PAP was coming from Chicago the following day. Would I collect her at Shannon?

She wasn't beautiful but she was disquieting. She made me feel I was missing the point all the time. Her black sweater was emblazoned with a large purple and blue peacock. She filled the car with her scent and intellect. There was no air to breathe. We talked about her Ph.D. thesis on George Russell and feminism. She was also a poet, interested in the idea of absence. She wanted to write on the Famine in Ireland. Not on those who died or emigrated but on those who were left behind.

She clutched a large, shiny radio set on her knees. We stopped several times to get a converter for it. The radio was more important than anything. It was a gift to Bernard. It had long wave, medium wave, short wave and ultra-short. She said that she and Bernard had been in communication since the age of four. They spoke to each other by short-wave radio.

She never saw Bernard. His life and love dissolved in Paxil. He was dozed and dazed. He felt a new tide of affection for his wife. She, in turn, forgave him for making a balls of his chances of ever becoming Dean of Arts. His children were brought to see him. He promised them all a trip to the Himalayas and instructed his solicitor to write a letter to the PAP.

She showed it to me.

'I must request that you cease to interfere in any way with the family life of my client. Further, I must demand that you put an end forthwith to all harassment and cease to libel the good name of Professor Slattery. If you do not comply with this request my client will be forced to take appropriate legal action against you.'

The PAP sent him by return a bill for $2,000 to cover her air fare, the cost of phone calls and the radio. Their accounts, like their love, were never to be settled.

These days I can't help looking up to Slattery with admiration. It was not until recently that I realised how adroitly he evades the drudgery of life. At the Christmas party, when he was bored with the conversation, he simply put his head on his arm and fell asleep. Nobody questioned his right to do so. The other day he gave a lecture. He stopped in the middle and went home. Everybody understood. And everybody does. No one says anything if he doesn't go to Faculty meetings, doesn't turn up for lectures, doesn't see students, doesn't look after his children, doesn't go to mass on Sundays. He spends five months of every year with the Maharishi Mahesh Yogi at Rishinkesh. He can get away with anything. He is the only free man I know.

A chomhairle féin do mhac Anna agus ní bhfuair sé riamh níos measa.

The Missionary

'Father Boniface, you're a real shit,' said the Abbot of Petra Fertilis.

Boniface couldn't but agree. He had betrayed God. He had fallen into grievous sin with a woman. Why he did it was a mystery to him. Most likely he had simply got tired of God's inexorable absence. And the Devil's absence for that matter. Whatever the reason, he fell in love with a woman in white who sat beside him on the plane from Heathrow to Dublin. She chanted, 'Good morning Father' with a little chuckle in her voice and he said, 'Good morning Miss,' and felt that the world had come to a stop. He fell in love with her just like that, from the very first word. He fell in love with her because she was warm and beautiful and her amber eyes said, 'Boniface you're a lovely man.'

God never said it. Nor did the Devil.

The Abbot's jibes bounced off Boniface like dried peas. As a matter of fact, they brought him solace. Maybe

God was real after all, at least for the Abbot. He must be if He could inspire such bluster. But then, people tended to fantasise about things which lay beyond their reach. They created myths about them. The Abbot, for example, made a big fuss about sex. Maybe he made a big fuss about God as well?

'You committed the most heinous of carnal sins straight after your ordination. The sacred oils were scarcely dry on your palms when you started fiddling with . . . I won't enquire into the details of your fall. But obviously you can't stay here any longer. You're a scandal to the Order. I'm sending you back to Curragreen.'

Boniface fell in love with the woman after eight years of monastic life. During all those years he hadn't read a single newspaper, hadn't listened to the radio and hardly spoke to his confrères. He didn't even know who was playing in the All-Ireland Finals. He was surrounded by men of profound piety. They were like dozy submarines. They surfaced from the abyss with their periscopes aloft. Cursorily they inspected the horizon, spoke solemn words of benediction or rebuke, and submerged once again into the fathomless deeps. Among them Boniface learned Greek, Latin, Spanish, Detachment and Restraint. Each morning he whipped the flesh into submission and emptied himself of himself to make the more room for God. About women he knew only this: the holier the woman, the more she is a woman.

Like Teresa of Avila for example. She had mystical raptures and the Devil appeared to her on a regular basis. Nothing like that had ever happened in Petra Fertilis. No revelations, no signs in heaven, no celestial trumpets, no trials, no wanton breasts and buttocks shape-shifting on

the quilt, no, not even on the night before Boniface's
ordination.

Boniface didn't really know what to make of life in the
monastery. He was neither bored nor excited. It was the
only life he knew. Obediently he rose at three o'clock in
the morning for prayers and flogged his shoulder blades,
left and right and left again. Thereafter he slid from
matins to lauds, from none to terce. He and his confrères
moved through the order of the day like a shoal of
migrating mackerel.

Boniface was amazed at the naturalness of his sin. And
the depth of it. And the agony of it. And the beauty of it.
And the guilt of it. Here he was, going to the altar in the
morning, hearing confession, giving absolution and
thinking of the endless lies he had to tell in order to see
the woman in the white pleated skirt and the white silk
blouse. The few times they were together they loved each
other as if the next day they were to be cast into hell.
They were horrified by their sin and thrilled by the
horror of it. Especially Boniface. For the woman in white
was much more practical than him. She wrote a letter
which went: 'Boniface, *a grá*, I can't be flying forever
from London to Dublin to meet you in the lounge of the
Shelbourne. We can't go on like this. Do something, for
God's sake.'

So Boniface applied to the London School of Econo-
mics to take a course in sociology and thereby add to his
Order's wisdom and learning. His superiors in Rome
liked the idea but thought that the London School of
Economics was a pagan institution and proposed
Louvain instead. For the first time in his life Boniface

dug his heels in and said: No, he wasn't interested, thank you very much.

For the first time too the woman in white lost patience with him. She wept as she hung above him: 'Boniface, you should have fought harder for me. You don't know how to fight for things. You've got bone lazy in the service of God. You're a nincompoop.'

Boniface agreed – but what could he do?

When London was gone he understood that his slide towards perdition had come to an end. So he went to the Professor of Divinity to ask him what to do. He put all his cards fair and square face up on the table. The Professor looked at them aghast. He was used to dealing with problems of spiritual aridity and self abuse. But this?

He needed to clarify a few quick points. Was Boniface's mother still alive? And his father – what sort of relationship had Boniface with him? Was the woman in question a Catholic? Did he employ prophylactic devices, singly or in combination? Had they engaged in unnatural acts together? How often?

'My dear Brother in Christ,' the Professor said at last, 'you must see your Superior and lay it all before him, just as you laid it before me.'

Then he blessed Boniface and prayed that he be granted the gift of tears.

So Boniface went to see the Abbot. We know what the Abbot had to say. As a punishment for breaking the vows of Poverty, Chastity and Obedience, he sent Boniface back to his old novitiate in Kerry, down to Curragreen at the world's end. There Boniface was to teach Greek, say mass, reflect on his wickedness but on no account hear confession or preach. The will of his Superior was the will of God. So Boniface went to the world's end hoping to mend his vocation.

The woman in white didn't give up easily. Every week she sent Boniface a tightly folded copy of *The Times Literary Supplement* with a letter discreetly pasted within. One day Father Superior snatched the *TLS* out of Boniface's cell to horrify himself with a favourable review of *Is Ireland Dying?* Needless to say what happened next. He had never seen a love-letter before. It was his duty to read it and read it he must. To tell the truth he was a bit disappointed. But debauchery was debauchery, look at it how you will.

There was only one place left for Boniface: Lisgorm Abbey, the Alcatraz of the White Friars in Ireland. There he was given a small dark cell with a narrow bed, a chair, a table and a crucifix. On no account was he to think of, write to, or make any contact whatsoever with the weaker sex. Once in a while, however, he was allowed a visit from his sister who brought him second-hand books on fishing and packages of Earl Grey tea. They went for long walks together on the cliff tops with the Atlantic Ocean gulping and regurgitating beneath them.

When it was discovered that Boniface didn't have a sister he was summoned by Father Provincial. The Provincial asked him only one question: 'Father Boniface, how would you like to go to the Philippines?'

What was Boniface to say? He said: 'Father Provincial, it is not what I like, I think it is what you want.'

He was pleased with the symmetry of his reply.

(2)

Before going on his mission to the Orient, Boniface was

granted freedom of movement. He wasn't moving for very long when he was spotted by Lucy O'Toole. She was out walking along the Clarin River when she saw Boniface sitting on the bank with a woebegone fishing rod drooping over the stream.

'So beautiful and yet so sad,' she thought.

How could she have known that Boniface was fishing for his last trout in Ireland, looking for the last time at the river, at the ruins of the castle beyond and at the little Irish colleen coming down the path towards him in the twilight?

With the desperate courage of the exile Boniface whispered: 'Good evening, Miss.'

His face among the flaggars brought a lump to her throat. Something about the hurt in his eyes, something about his lanky dark hair as in portraits of Robert Emmet in the Dock, something about the way he said 'Miss' melted her insides. There was a dead trout beside him on the grass. To cover her lust she burst out with an 'Ohhh look! What a lovely fish!'

'Rose-moles all in stipple upon trout that swim,' Boniface recited, running his finger lovingly along the flank of the fish.

Lucy hunkered down beside him. He told her that when you landed a trout it was gold vermilion for a millimetre of a second and you would never see that gold vermilion again.

After dinner with Boniface, Lucy couldn't get to sleep. All night she looked at him out of the corner of her eyes. Now and then she ran her finger down his thigh and whispered what you might expect: 'My weeny weeshy golden trout.'

Three days later she sat beside him on the plane on the first leg of his journey to Manila.

'I want to look at you till Rome,' she said, and wouldn't listen to his gentle protest. She was like Boniface's mother the time he was in the seminary. Every three months his little Irish mother made the long journey by train to visit him down in Curragreen. She would walk the seven miles from the station with her bags full of apple tarts and blackcurrant jam made specially for him. She would come panting up the steps of the monastery and collapse at the door with exhaustion and excitement. How she wanted to cuddle her little man again! Once, in her agitation, she let her bags fall in the hallway and broke all the jam jars. Everything had to be fed to the seminary hens. She would see Boniface for just one hour because he couldn't be late for five o'clock prayer. Then off she went the seven miles back to the train.

Lucy was just like that.

When they said goodbye to each other in the Piazza Santa Maria Maggiore Boniface felt relieved. But when he soared skyward over Fumicino the sun was setting in the Mediterranean and he wished he were going down with it.

(3)

Boniface was assigned to a monastery in the middle of nowhere on the tiny island of Villo Nillo. His new Father Superior, a MacCarthy from Cork, forbade him to visit the village, to talk to strangers or to imagine for a moment that he was on the Costa del Sol. But we know Boniface by now. He didn't protest, but the very next day he slipped out of the monastery. Out in the barrios, under the nipa palms, he listened to the myriads of humming cicadas and the call of the geckos. He was surrounded by smiling eyes and lips to which he said 'How d'y do' in his most courtly manner. Half-starved children with coconut faces came up to him to teach him the words for 'water', 'sky', 'sun' and 'rich man'. Their hands, when they touched his face, smelled of pineapple. Their words seeped through him like honey. Boniface was dumbfounded. Having committed grave sin with full knowledge and full consent he had been cast into Paradise. Where was the logic? Where was the justice?

At Easter Boniface was sent to Bacolod, the island of sugar and spice. There he preached his first sermon on love to the hacienderas. Pure blooded women came to his retreat in their best silks and jewels and most devastating perfumes. After the Gospel, Boniface led a little girl up from the front pew, placed her beside him on the altar with his arm round her shoulders and took as his text:

'Jerusalem, Jerusalem, how often would I have gathered your children under my wing like a hen her chicks but you would not!'

He told his congregation how his little Irish mother looked after the chickens and goslings, what care she took to keep them warm in a shoe-box by the hearth, how there was always one chick that wanted to go astray and how she would hunt round the kitchen and under the dresser for it with the handle of a broom. So it was with God and us.

The ladies gazed at him in a soft, pliant rapture. Boniface felt his chest begin to phosphoresce under the gold and white of the chasuble. He was full of vim and the Holy Spirit. His voice caressed their ripe souls.

Cadence after cadence he drew them further and further from the opulent haciendas where they languished with their adulterous husbands and promiscuous maids.

'This little girl beside me, this innocent child in her pigtails and pink bows, is an image of that sweetness which all of you, all without exception, feel deep down in your hearts. As Father Gerard Manley Hopkins put it: "There lies the dearest freshness deep down things." And it is deep down that the Great Lover touches us.'

After mass one of the ladies got up and approached Boniface. As she swung towards him up the aisle she unclasped a string of pearls from her neck and stripped her arms of silver bracelets.

'In grateful appreciation for what you have said to us, Father.' She smiled and handed him the jewels.

Her name was Imelda.

Imelda was perfect. She had the face of an infanta, the erudition of a savante and the affluence of a cacique. Her life was full of exquisite people, objects and ideas. Her husband came from the bluest of the blue-blooded *illustrados*, her underwear and shoes from the best couturiers in Paris and her views on love from *Le Petit Prince* by Saint-Exupéry.

Imelda liked the classical side of Boniface, his Roman nose, chiselled thin lips and his shy quotations from the Greek and Latin poets. She had a precise idea of what an innocent romance should be like in order to be more than chaste and less than sinful. She shed enchantments about her and left them to ripen in the air. She was a scent, a promise, a feel-of-primrose touch which settled on Boniface's thighs in the most exquisite unfulfilment.

All of a sudden countless blessings and favours were

showered on the Master of Villo Nillo. The Lord, as he said himself, looked kindly upon him. He was now a freelance preacher, no longer attached to monastery, abbey or church. He was flown from island to island to give retreats and to be fêted by the ladies of the archipelago. Wherever he went, people dropped everything and rushed to abandon themselves to the word of God. Gathered about him they became one body responsive to every thrust and tremolo of his voice. They wept and moaned and laughed in unison. In gratitude they sent him baskets of mangoes, pineapples, sweet potatoes and manioc. The ladies threw cocktail parties at which they gave away their pearls.

'Is it me?' wondered Boniface, rather unnecessarily. For let us be clear: it was not his will to be pampered and admired and exalted but the will of a people craving for love.

When Boniface received a summons to present himself before the Cardinal Archbishop, he stumbled to the Palace as if to the gallows.

'Sacred Heart of Jesus', he repeated, 'I place all my trust in Thee.'

Had His Eminence heard about his liaison with Aga or Mimi or Florence? Or Zuna? Zuna was a rich widow with five children, seven servants and a neo-Gothic mansion. She was an avalanche of dark hair, joy and impatience. She insisted that Boniface move into her residence in Luneta Gardens where he could refresh himself daily in her blue marble swimming-pool. Boniface wondered if it wouldn't be better to meet at his place but she said, 'Corazon, it's too late for scruples. Can't you see – you've already gone native!'

She read Boniface's fortune in the tea leaves and told him he had a golden future. And yet, in spite of the good augury, Boniface walked to the Cardinalature rehearsing a humble confession and planning a firm purpose of amendment.

His Eminence was most agreeable. He presented Boniface with a tray of drinks and cheroots and came to the point at once: 'Father Boniface, we have heard glowing reports of your work for the *cursillios*. How would you like to administer the Diocese? Everything will be placed in your hands.'

Though Boniface in his amazement and gratitude and relief said neither yes nor no, the Cardinal took it that he had said yes.

The ladies of Manila were delighted. Insatiable in their generosity, they furnished him with a panelled office and boardroom in the centre of town. He had three secretaries and nothing much to do. The Cardinal thought the world of him and invariably called him in for consultation before meeting with his own council of Monsignori. Boniface was judicious, impartial and wise. He was never so forward as to give his own opinion but deployed instead quotations from the classical authors and the English Catholic poets. Everybody who was anybody noticed how His Eminence's speeches improved after Boniface took over.

Apart from Boniface and the Cardinal's speeches, things were not quite right in Manila. The slum dwellers of Tonda lost patience with their poverty. One minute they were smiling and singing, the next they were cursing and rioting. The socialists lost patience with the *illustrados*. And the students began to agitate because they had lost patience with practically everything. The more impatient ones began to disappear. Their mangled, swollen corpses turned up in the corners of cane fields or festered in the reed beds of rivers. After the massacre in Monte-lupa the students surrounded the Cardinal's Palace and called him an imperialist lackey. 'Out, out, out, fascist lout!', they chanted and drew swastikas on the walls. They had a list of ten demands.

The Cardinal and the Monsignori assembled in the Chapter Hall. Some were for calling the Constabulary, others wanted to bring in the Civilian Home Defence Force, still others were confused. Finally, they turned to the only white man present and asked him what to do.

'Somebody should go out and talk to these people,' said Boniface.

'Would you do it?' asked the Cardinal.

'I'd be delighted, Your Eminence.'

So Boniface sauntered down to the students in the blistering sun and asked them if they would like to delegate a small group to join him for a chat. When the *ad hoc* committee was elected, Boniface brought them all to a coffee shop and bought them ice cream.

Seated around wobbly pyramids of vanilla and pista-chio garnished with cherries and molten chocolate, they discussed the ten demands. To and fro the argument went. The revolutionaries were impressed by Boniface's courtesy and consideration. Never before had they been treated with such kindness. The opened their hearts to him. After opening their hearts they stopped making a fuss and went home. In this way Boniface delayed the Philippine revolution by a good ten years.

Manila was at his feet. Fine wines, glorious women,

objets d'art and power honed his spirit and subtilised his mind. All the dross was drained from him. His face acquired a look of refined benevolence and his gait a patrician pace. Sermons on love mellowed his voice and brought out its alluvial tones. He was immaculate in his white linen suit and lemiscular straw hat. All the harder, then, to believe the rumours that swept through the Confraternities and the Golf Clubs. Father Boniface was leaving the priesthood and returning to Ireland!

How could this be? Imelda claimed that the heat and humidity had got to him in the end. Aga insisted that it was all because of the white woman Lucy who had come to Manila to torment him. Anybody could see that she fed on darkness and denial, that woman with her long face and dirty hair.

No, said Mimi, it was something else. It was because of the other Irish priest, the one who was organising the *campenseros* on the islands and preaching revolution in the name of Christ. Father Boniface didn't like him. How could he like a man who spread hatred and division rather than love and harmony?

The Cardinal Archbishop had his own explanation. Boniface was leaving because he wanted the image of the priesthood to remain unsullied.

Zuna did not believe any of these stories. She had seen it all coming. She had been reading the tea leaves for weeks and couldn't discover a pattern any more in Boniface's cup. She saw nothing but mess and muddle.

At the farewell reception in the garden of the Papal Nunciature, Boniface excelled himself. For the first time in years he was wearing a tailor-made black suit and Roman collar. They went extraordinarily well with his deep coppery tan. Standing on the terrace with a gin in his hand and a shy smile on his lips he spoke of what a difference the Philippines had made to his life, how much he had learned, what tidings of this gracious, kindly people and gentle land he would bring back with him to Europe. *Vale, aeternum valeque.* It was impossible not to be in love with our dear hidalgo *irlandes*, said Imelda presenting him with an inscribed diary on behalf of the Manila Praesidium of the Legion of Mary.

Only Zuna was uneasy. She watched him like a condor. She could accept his going away. These things happened to women. It was something else that bothered her. At first glance he seemed all of a piece and in complete control. But then, if you were a woman and looked closer, you saw that he was a little vague, a little careless, a little scattered. Why was one of his silver cufflinks missing? Why hadn't he brushed the dandruff from his shoulders? Why was it that the colour of his socks didn't quite match? There was something odd too about his behaviour. While chatting away with Imelda, Boniface was simultaneously smiling at the Cardinal and being stern with the American Ambassador. It was as if different bits of him were going off in different directions. This was what perturbed Zuna as they stood in the Nuncio's garden ablaze with orchids, smiling, sweet-scented Monsignori and beautiful bra-less women.

Even if we wanted to end the story of Boniface's vocation on this mildly disturbing note, we cannot. We have to follow it to the bittersweet end.

(4)

When he returned to Ireland, Boniface didn't propose to Lucy and they didn't live happily ever after. He didn't go back to his family and there was no fatted calf slaughtered to celebrate the prodigal's home-coming. Neither did he repent and submit to the discipline of his Order. He did everything upside down and in spite of himself. He went to Galway where nobody knew him and nobody was waiting for him. For ten pounds a week he rented a converted garage with second-hand rickety furniture and a carpet that stank of cat's piss and vomit.

Day after day he sat up in bed watching the fat rain drops splatter on the window and warp the unkempt street beyond. His eyes followed the women on their way to mass or to the supermarket. He had the Manila diary with a page for every day by his bed. It was blank except for one entry under 17 March:

> Their faces have the pallor of cold bedrooms.
> They wear their womanhood inside out, with
> the seams and loose threads showing. Their
> lips, unkissed for centuries, have grown
> vestigal and narrowed into cicatrices.

Boniface got up only when night fell. If the moon and the stars were out he walked the bohereens eating hamburgers and chips from a paper bag. At other times he rose just before dawn. For an evanescent moment, as he watched the gashes of red and yellow and green in the east, he stood shot through with wild excitement. Then he half-raised his left hand in shy benediction. But when the light grew and greyed and the bungalows along the

Barna road brazenly reasserted themselves, he turned for home, a stray mongrel at his heels.

Not every night was bright or starry and more often than not the dawnlight was smothered in rain. On such mediocre nights Boniface took to hunting cats. The best place was the Fish Market near the Spanish Arch. After the pubs in High Street had closed and the drunks had gone home or collapsed in doorways, the cats came out to mate or scavenge in the parking lot. Enter Boniface and the dog over O'Brien's Bridge pretending to be ordinary passers-by. All of a sudden Boniface turns round, slips the dog off the leash and shouts: 'Attaboy Magnus! Go for it! Nail the cunts!'

Magnus shoots off as if discharged from a catapult. The cats scatter, miaowing hysterically. They leap on cars. They summersault over rubbish bins. Once beyond Magnus's reach they snarl and spit down at him. Boniface takes over and drives them off the car bonnets with his umbrella. Again the chase begins.

It could go on like that for hours until Magnus and Boniface and the cats were exhausted. Magnus savaged an average of two cats per week. Boniface kept a careful score in the 'annoplanning' section of his big diary.

One such morning at 3 a.m. a squad car swung into the Fish Market and drew up beside Boniface. The sergeant rolled down the window and opened the back door.

'Sit in there like a good man,' he said. 'You must be sodden with the rain and the cold.'

Magnus raced desperately after the car all the way to Abbeygate Street. Then he gave up.

(5)

Nobody knew what happened to Boniface after he was caught cat hunting by night in Galway. He disappeared for years and years. Some said he went back to the Philippines. Others insisted that they had seen him at Galway Races in the company of a young man. Then one day Father Conmee of Petra Fertilis discovered him in Our Lady's Hospice for the Dying curled up in bed and a shadow of himself. When he spoke to him, Boniface replied in Latin which Fr. Conmee had long ago forgotten.

The next evening two young postulants of the Order arrived to sit with their dying confrère. They freshened up his pillows, stroked his head and held his hand. Boniface lay there mute and impassive while they spoke to him gently. Father Conmee had told them that the dying can hear everything that is said to them.

Every evening thereafter two students from Boniface's Order were sent to sit with him. They watched him with a mixture of awe and curiosity. They had been told only as much as they needed to know. Father Boniface was one of their men who had been broken on the mission field. They too might one day be broken. Every so often the night nurse popped in with a cup of tea for the lads, nodded her head at the shadow in the bed and whispered: 'It can't be long now.'

But it was. Four weeks passed and Father Boniface was still faintly breathing and still listening in silence to the postulants. They were getting bored with the long vigils by his bedside. It was Lent and they had extra prayers and fasting to do. When they asked the Houseman what was the likely prognosis he said that the poor creature should have been dead long ago but was taking it at his own pace.

As it happened, it was a liturgical pace.

On Holy Thursday Boniface's breath grew harsh. On Good Friday his fingers clenched and unclenched the bedspread. On Holy Saturday he sat up. On Easter Sunday he began to speak.

At first it was difficult to catch his words. But as the night wore on he gained in strength and clarity. He spoke about love. Alarmed, the students by his bedside called the nurse. She tried to hush him but he only spoke with greater animation. Then, just as suddenly as he had begun, he stopped and fell back into a stupor. The Houseman said it was surely the last kick of a dying animal.

But it wasn't. The following night he roused himself again. And the next night. And the next. With the help of the students he would sit up in bed, smile shyly at his unseen listeners, scratch his head with a crooked finger and begin: 'What on earth are we going to talk about today? Good Lord, I haven't prepared a thing. But here goes anyway.'

The fame of his sermons spread through the Hospice, back to Curragreen and to the Convent of the Sisters of Charity. Nurses coming off duty hung around the wards waiting for him to start. The nuns rearranged their evening prayers to witness the miracle. Clerical students came in droves on their bicycles. Father Boniface's bed had to be transported to the assembly room where every evening at nine o'clock folding chairs were brought in and a candle lit before the statue of the Sacred Heart.

The nuns laid on ham sandwiches and tea. Excitement grew in the Hospice corridors. Would he be able for it tonight? And for how long? No one could tell if Father Boniface would speak for half an hour, half the night or die. The Houseman said that the whole thing was obscene. It was getting too much like Russian roulette. But Boniface himself disagreed.

'Some people break into flower at seven years of age,' he said, 'and all the rest of their life is a waste. Some blossom at twenty, others at fifty. I had to wait until now to put out a few leaves and petals. Let me be.'

The Houseman's mistrust was shared by Father Conmee and the Director of Novices at Petra Fertilis. If in the past they had been envious of Boniface's life, now they were envious of his death. It was all a bit fishy. No, this time he wasn't going to be allowed to get away with it. They went to the Hospice to see for themselves.

When they arrived, Boniface had just been hoisted up in bed and his lips moistened with glycerine. He looked about him with tender affection and a shy smile flitted over his face.

'Good evening, ladies,' he said slowly.

'Good evening, Father,' replied the nuns, the nurses and, more hesitantly, the clerical students.

The Director of Novices was embarrassed. To him Boniface looked like a shorn old granny propped up in bed, making a show of herself.

While Boniface spoke, people nodded their heads and exchanged marvelling glances.

'Isn't he the real thing? Isn't he just?' they whispered.

It wasn't long before the Abbot and the Director of

Novices found themselves nodding away like everybody else, though a little more gravely.

It would spoil matters, in the cold light of day, to quote Boniface's sermon. Suffice to say that our two experts in the discernment of spirits found it uplifting, comforting and theologically sound. It brought them a strange kind of peace.

(6)

Boniface too was at peace. After those terrible nights of chasing Mimi across O'Brien's Bridge and up High Street and goading Imelda to despair in the Fish Market, he had finally come home. They were all sitting together again round the edge of Zuna's blue marble swimming-pool. The pool was full of glinting, glabrous goldfish. The ladies dipped delicate bronze feet in the water, nodding their heads and whispering to one another.

Boniface lay back in his deckchair and felt the happy fatigue of a job well done. His homily was over.

'Thank you for your attention, dear ladies,' he said. 'Tomorrow, *Deo volens*, we will meet again.'

He half raised two fingers of his left hand.

> '*Benedicat vos omnipotens Deus
> Pater,
> et Filius
> et Spiritus Sanctus.
> Amen.*'

In ainneoin na sagart, siad na daoine féin a chruthaigh formhór na Naomh.

The Man Who Ate the Universe

In my life-chart Neptune is the real McCoy. It's hitting lots of planets. Neptune means heroin, alcohol, wanking and disillusion as well as the desire for transcendence.

I've always wanted to be a big Neptunian awash with the green waters of oblivion. I've this enormous desire for the wide, green, melting ocean which is the sign of the absolute. What I want is a life like a dream. That's what I really want. That's why I like alcohol, I like colour television, I like a warm bed on a winter's morning and that kind of stuff. Don't get me wrong. My desire is for reality. Not for a mirage but big juicy reality. We've got to let the juice and the sap ejaculate over the world, we've got to see it gushing over everything like a geyser.

My biggest disappointment is the sort of brain I've been given. It's a brain whereby I can only work on two levels. I can work on the flat land. I can lick stamps or cork bottles or carry televisions. I can do the most menial and mechanical jobs and I like those jobs because I cannot fail at them. Or I can work on the absolute icy pin-prick mountain tops where very few people can survive.

There I discover the exact Irish origin of Hamlet, there I discover the secret of the Boyne code, the key to John Dee's alchemical symbolism, Sweet Jesus, even the principle of realism in quantum mechanics. I discover things that nobody has copped on to before. But I can't work in the middle regions of the inbred, equine wankers, the academic Coca-Cola salesmen with their money, their statutes and their long dreary holidays with the wife and two kids in Brittany.

I tried everything. I licked stamps. I wrote rock operas. I studied physics. I read relativity theory. I learned how to draw, to play the guitar. I did three-dimensional work in the Art College. I sold insurance. I took teaching jobs. I went round the twist. I tried everything. I was forced into menial jobs, the ultimate shame. I can't describe the shame of it. For years, on and off, I carried televisions for a rental company, up to ten thousand televisions!

It broke me. My mother kept saying: 'You are the most unfortunate poor soul I ever came across. Worse than a case of multiple sclerosis.' She kept pressing: 'Well, three months have passed, six months, two years, six years and now when are you going to get yourself a decent professional job?'

I didn't have the brain for it! If I did a computer programmer's test, I'd fail it. I only have the brains to discover things that only Einstein could discover. It's so horrible that it's comical.

It was written into my chart that I would become professionally disastrous at the age of twenty-eight. As the Saturn Return came around – and Saturn comes around when you are twenty-eight or twenty-nine and your life is shattered – I collapsed. I've met several people who were driven all the way to the brink by the Saturn Return. I've looked up my chart. I had five or six squares that year. Massive squares from massive planets. Now one square can kill you and I had five and I could have strangled people with my bare hands during that year. I was tortured, I was put through the fires of hell. Nineteen years of crucifixion, of third-rate academic results, of endless sweat and labour when people felt – and I felt – I could have been a Master!

I began to slide and slide until I crashed. On the day of my breakup, Uranus was right in my zenith and Kairon, the Christ plant, which was only discovered in 1977, was exactly opposed to it at the nadir. That was the day! Palpitations, terrible pain in the gut, absolute burn out. I haven't recovered yet.

There was something wrong up there. I'm not gonna be bothered describing it to you. You're not gonna be told. I won't talk about pain, I'll talk about something worse. Eating snot. Eating snot from a pimple three times a week. I'm putting that image deliberately and delicately to you to let you feel what disgust and nausea is about. Do you like that? You call that challenge? Do you think that spending the whole day humping around Galway trying to collect my fecking disability benefit is the right thing for the only man in Ireland – no, Europe – who understands John Dee and Bernard Lonergan?

Look at this rat-infested hole with the wind and the rain coming under the door, with no cooker bar a primus stove and a sleeping bag instead of a bed. Do you think I like it? Do you think that it stirs the celestial realm of my brain?

But I'm not going to move. Not yet. This place is

central. My life is organised here. I wake up at eight and I make myself a lot of hot water mixed with ginger and a pear juice. Then I do my asanas and then I go back to bed for ten minutes. Then I meditate. Then I start chopping carrots for my dinner and it takes me a lot of time to get my dinner together. For almost an hour I have to recover from eating. I can't even read a newspaper after dinner. My arm is fucked from lifting the spoon. That's what exhausts me. That's why I can't speak. I don't know why it has to happen to people.

I don't know why I wasn't allowed to be married and join a squash club when I was twenty-two and a half. Once upon a time I was living at home, I had a car, a colour television and a stamp collection. I had respect-ability. But because of my chart – and there's no other explanation – I was not destined to hold on to them. I worked in the Post Office in Gort for eight years. The message was obvious – nothing's gonna happen, you were born, you're gonna have forty years of torture, you're gonna die. Dreadful.

After I quit my job there was this gigantic vacuum. I had to look good, I had to have respectability, I wanted to be able to explain my life to people who asked me what I was doing. That's why I thought of university. It was part of a Neptunian adventure. But I was scared to go to Dublin, scared like you might be scared to go to Tokyo. I had a very slow gestation. I arrived in Dublin, red-hot pokers in my hand. I had to be driven out of my red-hot pokers. My hand wouldn't let go off those bars until they grew white hot. And only when the flesh burned off and nothing but the bones remained and the bones were going black, would I let go.

When I eventually got into Trinity I thought it was glorious. Which it was, but only for a short period. My answers at exams were usually atrocious. I had to struggle against enormous barriers, enormous failure, enormous personal incompetence. It was a terrible mortification to find out that I couldn't work out the timetable, I couldn't put form on an essay, I couldn't read the phonetic alphabet. But I saw all the movies and all the theatre plays, I went to the Joyce Week, I met Anthony Burgess in Dawson Street and I asked him if he was afraid of death. I could see in him a fellow Catholic approaching me. I could see that he knew what I meant, that I wasn't joking.

'I'm terrified, terrified,' he said. 'Dreadfully, dreadfully afraid. Do you know Graham Greene? Greene is terrified himself. That's why he wanted somebody to shoot him in Haiti or wherever it was. That's why he is tempting all those South American gangsters. He actually feels that if somebody kills him he'll be saved.'

That's what Burgess said. Those were his very words.

I always knew I was intended to have adventures. I was to meet glamorous, strange and exotic women. I met them all right, but they were all screwing somebody else. The first woman I went to bed with was the ex-mistress of one of the Great Train Robbers. She was screwing a wrestler at the time. I was eighteen. It was dull, I was too brittle, I was too hard, I was too dried out. Existentially, she was a mediocre human being. Still, it was something, even if it was only an official hammer job.

I didn't get another screw for the next ten years. Not a thing. I had a sense of incredible nausea at the thought of having sex with somebody who might be like the girl next door. Or who might be a physical education teacher or an Irish teacher in Mary Immaculata up the road. On the other hand I knew that there was no bliss like looking forward to meeting a woman on a Friday evening after your week's work. You know that you can stay for the night, that there'll be rashers and eggs and sausages on the table the next morning. Jesus, I could cry when I think of it. That's why people get married.

I'll tell you why sex seems interesting to people.

We are born with a destiny. The destiny is bliss, absolute, sensuous, blissful carnal knowledge of the universe, fleshly union with all things. Power is not enough. You've got to have sex because it means transcending boundaries. Every fat oyster-eating arsehole knows as much.

I have an all-encompassing lust. I might be at a public meeting or writing notes about Cornelius Agrippa or reading *The Crane Bag* and all the time I'm thinking of sex. I can think about quantum mechanics and sex at the same time. That's because of the Neptunian influence. The brain is my erogenous zone. I want to puff it till it glows, I want to exhale it out of the top of my head like smoke, I want the dendrites to hum, I want the old jellyfish to have an orgasm.

I never wanted a Platonic relationship with a woman. I wanted a Plutonic one! There's a great line in *Catch 22* when the guy says, 'Remember when you were fifteen years old and the summer holidays were ten thousand years long and the nearest thing to heaven was an unhooked brassière?' Jesus, the guy put his finger on it.

But I had a coarse attitude to sex. There is this machine and we must do the job. Let's put machine into action, let's get figures up, let's see how far and how long and at how many angles. I had sex with a lot of women medidators, including women sidhas. I've probably had more all around screwing and messing with women meditators and sidhas and T.M. teachers than any living human being. But I enjoyed sex with only six women. Three of them were Monkeys. The other three were Goats. I enjoy the Monkeys and the Goats, there's something meek and aesthetic about them. All the rest was just official date stamping, notches on the crotch.

The most horrible experience was meeting a beautiful Capricorn with the pale skin of a queen of Connemara and huge round eyes and porter black hair. Everything, her face, the severe paleness of her skin, the hypocritical chastity of her black transparent dress and her super-rich accent made me feel so humid, so nervous that I backed up. I told myself that I was not interested in her, but I knew that I was making it up. She went for me because she thought that I was a natural middle-class Edwardian.

Normally women feel that I'm a harmless, innocent creature who thinks he has It for stirring his tea. But this one sank her teeth in my neck and said: 'Have you met a vampire before, darling?'

The first night I spent with her I found that I had no human feelings whatsoever. Just like that. I was going through the motions, like screwing a lump of snow. I should have enjoyed her because she was multiorgasmic, but I didn't. For some reason I wasn't interested in the skin and there should be interest in the skin, in the fingertips running over it, touching it and yet not touch-ing. If I feel that urge, I know I am into happiness and into contact. If I feel that urge, I know I am into happiness and into contact. If I don't feel that, I might just as well be licking a whitewashed cottage.

But on the second night a John Lennon record was on. He was singing that song, 'No mother-fucking something/dizzy Lizzy/tricky Dicky,/Just give me some Truth!'

It was fantastic! The record was going and I was going, it was like the cameras had been turned on, this was Jack Nicholson, this was fun! It wasn't like beating off in the jacks, not like a night job reading paperbacks under the scummy yellow light. It was the cinematic screw. It was good, it was like being a Big Boy. Ayyyyyyy, break the stars!

I know this kind of bliss can last maybe two weeks. Then it's going to be ripped away from me. The Capricorn fucked off. First she reassured me that I was bound for glory and then she left me after ten days. I was shattered that night. I deserve a break, I thought. I spent so many years on my own and then it's always wretched away from me. Back to scowering around pubs, going to desperate parties, draining the dregs of endless pints of Guinness, chatting up endless women, just to get what? Another two weeks? What a God-fecking-mighty awful existence!

When she left I put an ad in *Hot Press* 'An Aquarian looking for a female companion, preferably a Monkey or Goat.' You're not gonna guess who replied. She replied! The pale Capricorn! We met in Naughton's pub in Quay Street to talk things over and the next thing what do I see? The bitch throws herself at this journalist who's down from Dublin to investigate what the *New York Times* calls the left bank of Galway. Sweet Jesus!

'Have you met a vampire before!' she asks this other guy and bites his ear. And then they go off in his car and leave me there with the blood running cold in my veins. But as luck would have it, while driving through Salthill they were rammed by the Irish Press van. They spent the night in the Regional Hospital in fecking separate wards while I was knocking off a post-grad student in botany. Ayyyyyyyyyyy!

It was horrifying. I wasn't getting anywhere and she wasn't getting anywhere. So I ended up in the lap of luxury. That's what I call it. You know – yodelling in the canyon. Cunnilingus – what you get when you cross Cunard with Air Lingus. Myself, I call it the lap of luxury. If that doesn't work, forget it.

Why do I go for stuff like the lap of luxury, archaeology, mythology, transcendence and colour movies? It's the Neptunian thing. It's like walking around a field on a rainy Sunday afternoon. It can be an awful penance but if you know it's an archaeological site, as inaccessible as sex, then you don't feel your socks getting wet.

On the whole I've been lucky. Sometimes there has been a gap of eight years, sometimes three years, but God rewarded me with a few marvellous fucks. I mean, the likes of me deserve some crumbs.

The majority of the women I screwed had social status of some sort. They were all admired or lusted after by other men. Like this Australian opera singer that Mick Jagger was trying to break the bleeding door to get into and Harold Bloom was after. *I* got her in the end. It was good. It was up-market. Because a good woman is a woman that other men want. The woman that the big bastards, the goddamn high fliers can't get, that's a good woman. They didn't get her. *I* got her! It made me feel like God. You can do it, Luke! You can do it! You're no worse than others. You may hunch your shoulders, you wear a grey mack, you wander round Galway looking like some fecking hen, you're an academic bespectacled arsehole that woman laugh at at bus-stops – but YOU CAN DO IT! You got a woman everybody's after. You just stand upright there boy because that's up-market, that's respectability.

God had been merciful. I got my piece of ass, what Apuleius called a Golden Ass. Do you remember Apuleius' description of seeing the Goddess? Oh my God – stop!

These days I have a problem with women because I deny them my essence. I have to protect my essence if I am to rise to cosmic consciousness. I can't go on spending myself around and that's why I wear these rudvaksha beads. They push the *siúcra* up from the balls to the brain.

I always knew I was meant to experience enlightenment, to see the bliss level, the Eucharistic level. One day in Barna Wood I saw the life force run up through the trees and suffuse everything. I tasted the horizon as far as the Aran Islands. I ate the Universe, big juicy gobs of it. Since then I've had the odd bit of witnessing, the odd bit of *soma*. I once remained fixated at a corner near the Augustinian church on a Sunday afternoon with the *Sunday Telegraph* under my arm contemplating the meaning of the word NOW for a solid hour. I couldn't move until I'd beaten the problem. I blissed out thinking how relativity and quantum mechanics and evolution could all be expanded into a beautiful clear Catholic rationalism.

You see this iron ring on my finger? Made from a horseshoe. With this ring I'll turn my life round, I'll defeat the rakshasas, I'll bring in my own personal Golden Age. Maharishi's Indian astrologers told me to wear it. I paid a bleeding one hundred and sixty quid for my chart when I didn't have a rex. They have the whole thing computerised.

'Neptune,' they said, 'Neptune is the cause, mister, good and bad. You must neutralise the bad with a ring from the shoe of a female horse. If you do this simple thing you will be a very wealthy man at the age of forty-two and if you want to you can marry at forty-two and a half.'

'But I don't want to get married,' I said.

'Mister, I'm telling you! If it is your wish you can marry at forty-two and a half. No before and no after.'

'Do you say it to everybody?'

'I am telling you what I'm reading mister so don't make me angry. And I'm telling you that you'll be a millionaire! The stars, mister, the stars, you're going to break the stars!'

So my story is that I went through years of staggering boredom through my twenties, years of training and torture in my thirties to be successful and blissful during my forties. For some reason God has taken care of me. He put me in the right place at the right time, he gave me the right amount of money, he gave me the right kind of TV programmes, mostly British ones. Now at last I've got the feeling of not not understanding.

Last week I held a woman's hand. It was like being

inside her because of all the *siúcra* going to my brain, all the sesame and the ghee and the milk and the honey and the meditation. At the same time I realised that I was satisfied with just holding her hand. Now with the redirected *siúcra* I'm in a mild state of bliss lots of the time. I eat nothing but Amrit Kalash. It costs forty bleeding quid a go but it's got forty-three herbs from the Himalayas. I do it to build myself up to the point when I can open my newspaper after dinner without causing myself physical hysteria and nightmares.

I think I'm moving up to a new plane altogether. The old optimism is rising, the eleven projects will be carried out within four years. I'm planning to write a piece about John Dee. I discovered that he was teaching something like transcendental meditation in the seventeenth century to transform the crowned heads of Europe and to change the society.

I'm doing exactly what Dee was doing. I'm approaching politicians, especially Progressive Democrats. I feed Amrit Kalash to Unionists. My dharma in Ireland is to be right here right now.

I bet relativity, I bet quantum mechanics, I worked out what's wrong with the theory of natural selection, what's wrong with identifying the mind with the brain and what's wrong with nationalism. I can handle all that stuff. I have become a magus, a polymath – not on the surface, mind you – I've got right down to the basic knotty guts of things through mystic epistemology. I'm an applied hyromorphologist. I'm many things. That's what a double Aquarian is. I want to be something on which no name can be put. I'm gonna fuck the universe without having to commit a mortal sin. Ayyyyyyy, I'm gonna break the stars!!

Trí shaghas inchinne atá ann, - inchinn chloiche, inchinn cheurach, agus inchinn shrotha.

In the Company of Frauds

(1)

Sesame O'Hara was a poor hoor. She had spent the most wretched twenty years of her life at the University in Galway explaining and obfuscating the work of Irish writers, A.T. Harrington among them.

For all these years she suffered the birth pangs of a theory that poetry was not, as the best French critics had it, phallic/priapic but rather vaginal/Venusian. The fruit of her labour was a foetus in formalin, a study of Irish poetry from Alice Milligan to A.T. Harrington entitled *The Well and the Pump*. The book never got beyond the proof stage. Sesame chopped and changed it constantly. She kept expanding the vulvar aspects and contracting the phallic and then by turns expanding the phallic and contracting the vulvar.

Few of her students were impressed by her search for perfection. The majority were sure that she no longer knew her arse from her elbow. One Christmas they sent her a green-veined dildo made of Connemara marble in a black velvet box. O'Hara prayed to St. Sesaimh of Kinvara (anglicised Sesame) for release.

She always felt guilty. The vulvar theory was much against the grain of her Catholic upbringing. She would blush when asked to explain the gist of her research. More and more she was troubled by the indecency of her subject. Less and less was she able to endure the parasitism of her profession. The poet A.T. Harrington, for example, was a tree. She was the ivy. That's what occurred to her as she retyped for the umpteenth time her chapter 'The Modality of Desire in Harrington's Recent Verse'.

It was Harrington's oeuvre that caused all the problems. His poetry bulged with male Irish thuggery and threatened to wreck her theory at every turn. She tried to subdue him with words like 'discourse', 'desire', 'semiosis' and *jouissance*'. All in vain. In spite of his extraordinary talent for inwardness, Harrington remained feral and stank.

One night after a meeting of the International Association for the Study of Anglo-Irish Literature (Austrian Section) O'Hara got drunk. She emptied a bottle of contaminated Klosterneuburger at a reception hosted by the governor of Styria in the last Rosicrucian palace in Europe. She sat in a baroque bay window all on her own. She felt full of wind, piss and quotations.

'Shame, Sesame, shame,' she quoted her father, 'you rump-fed ronion you.'

She found it increasingly difficult to think and speak without quoting somebody. She felt another quote coming on, this time from Harrington.

Suddenly it occurred to her that the quotation didn't

sound right. As a matter of fact it wasn't Harrington at all. It was her very own. That's how she discovered that she could write poetry.

That night she smoked forty Gitanes and wrote five better-than-Harrington poems.

She felt sick in the morning. But her mind was in a ferment. She declaimed aloud a page of Harrington and a sheet of O'Hara. She was delighted. Harrington's verses unstitched themselves down the page like old woollen socks. There were holes and runs in them. They betrayed a shameless indecision. Hers, by contrast, were diaphanous stockings. They had definite seams, an amber transparency, a feminine pungency.

(2)

Dear Sir,

Please find enclosed a sequence of poems inspired by recent events in Lebanon. They are a continuation of the work which you published last year in the spring issue of *Cosmos*.

Yours
Alan T. Harrington

This letter provoked one of the more vicious imbroglios in the recent history of Irish literature in English. It was concocted by Sesame O'Hara and it led to a curious vulvar period in the work of Harrington. The one-time eulogist of bed, booze, brothels and fornication in graveyards became the celebrant of Mother Gaia. She tightened her teeth on him and opened her swamps, her dark oozings seeping and softening his cough.

Sir,

What the hell do you think you're doing? I'll sue you for printing these abortions under my name in your last issue. Lebanon *my arse*.

A. Thurley Harrington

Harrington was to regret that letter for the rest of his natural life. Word of the appearance of a pseudo-Harrington reached *Horizon, The New York Review of Books, Encounter, The Clare Champion* and *Poetry Ireland*. All five rejected his just completed work on the grounds of uncertainty of authorship.

He tugged the hair that grew between his teeth. He cursed in Munster Irish. The famous bronchitis thickened in his chest. His coughing, spitting and sweating drove his lover away. But he was no fool. He had difficulty enough getting published as it was. Any further complications would shaft his chances of winning the American National Poetry Award. In the end he kicked for touch by pleading insanity.

Dear Sir,

Please, disregard my ill-tempered epistle of 21 May. In confidence I must tell you that I have had something of a breakdown and my left hand, so to speak, didn't know what my right hand was doing. The poems you published are, of course, mine, and herewith I enclose an epilogue to my Lebanon sequence. Such a sad country!

Yours,
A.T.H.

Harrington boomed. The Peace Movement invited him

to Acapulco to address a symposium on Suppressed Nationalities of the World; Swedish feminists elected him an honorary life member of the *Bara for Kvinnor Association* and he turned down the offer of a Doctorate of Literature (*honoris causa*) from University College Galway.

(3)

During this vulvar period of his work Harrington never once slept alone.

(4)

Sesame O'Hara wrote and wrote. Harrington, who hadn't read anything in twenty years, was faced with the distasteful task of rummaging through literary periodicals to find out what he had published. He couldn't make head or tail of his new work. He tried reading the critics for clarification. The critics said, for example: 'It follows that a central concern of his [Harrington] is the restoration of female energy to its appropriate position in the scheme of things, and, by the same token, the need for a transformation of male energy as we know it today. Here is the savage economy of hieroglyphics.'

This frightened him. He was fit to be tied.

The inevitable happened. That year the male coquettes of the International Association for the Study of Anglo-Irish Literature assembled in Munich for their quintennial conference. They needed one another. They needed Harrington.

He came in defiant Bermuda shorts and Palestinian shawl. He chaired the opening session and thereby managed to say nothing.

Professor Sesame O'Hara was there as well. When she saw Harrington she trembled and ran to the Fräuleins to check if her hair, her eyes, her cheeks and her lips were in their right places. She wanted to talk to him but it was impossible because of the innovative set-up of the conference. In the dining hall there were twelve tables. One of them was covered with a black table cloth. The others were in white. Anybody who sat at the black table was excused from talking or socialising in any way (the director of the conference got the idea from a café in Istanbul). Harrington sat at the black table.

Sesame invoked St Sesaimh of Kinvara who answered her prayer.

When nobody was looking she switched the tablecloth. Harrington, whose attention was focused on exploring inner space, didn't notice the difference. He sat in his usual place looking like Ho Chi Min before the fall of Saigon.

Sesame joined him and introduced herself.

'Hi, there, wanker,' he greeted her and slobbered his soup.

She stared at him, bottomified.

'Bollocks,' she breathed, frightened of herself.

Harrington was delighted. He offered her a glass of Madeira and a slice of lemon.

The IASAIL delegates who observed the encounter were pleasantly dismayed to see Harrington's bony hand crawl over Sesame's back and shoulders. A little later they watched the two of them shamble out of the dining hall swathed in muslined conversation.

Harrington's room stank of beer and incense. O'Hara struggled to turn their conversation to post-modernism.

But Harrington was randy. He bolted the door and shouted 'Open Sesame!' He started to poke at her which she found embarrassing. She could take *plaisir du texte* but not *plaisir de l'homme*.

In an effort to divert his attention and finally come to the point she started to praise his recent work. She would give an arm and a leg, her professorship even, to produce such stuff.

'Your professorshit!' exclaimed Harrington and released her. He had been drinking for days and felt like a full cistern in need of a good flush. It came in a torrent of green venom.

'Your professorshit,' he repeated. 'I've hardly written a thing for eight years.'

Sesame startled.

'How do you mean?' she enquired.

She had only been writing under his name for the previous fifteen months.

'I'm a fraud,' said Harrington, relishing his words. 'You see there's this creature writing my stuff better than I could ever do it myself.'

Sesame's heart stopped.

'Who's he?' she asked in a small voice.

'It's a she,' Harrington chuckled. 'Maisie MacMahon. A small farmer's wife in the County Leitrim with too much time on her hands. She isn't bad. But a year or so ago she developed this feminist kink. At first I wanted to stop her but then I thought, what's the use, a change is as good as a rest.'

Sesame gazed at him blankly, her mind dry and toxic as a puff-ball.

'I'm a fraud,' repeated Harrington with glee. 'But she's got what it takes. What odds: every man should have a smart woman like that in his life.'

Is fearr beagán don ghaol ná morán don aitheantas.

O'Sullivan in the
Luxembourg Gardens

'J'aimerais une verre de la bierre, s'il vous plaites,' I said to a waitress on the terrace of Le Dôme.

I said it and wondered what was wrong with the sentence. Every time I spoke French it felt like standing in front of a doctor and being examined for the clap. I was ashamed. My words were inflamed and ulcerated. Giselle said that it was because my mind was totally unfocused. She advised me to take Vitamin B Complex every morning. But the vitamins didn't seem to help. Nothing helped.

The slinky black puma of a waitress gave me a look.

'Are you English?' she asked in English.

'Au contraire,' I replied, blushing .

It was very pleasant to be Irish in Paris at that time. I was pastoral, romantic and dangerous, like the characters in *Taxi Mauve*. I was reckless and ungovernable. I had secret dealings with the IRA. Even my bad French was a sign of innate defiance. I loved music and alcohol and, despite my rugged appearance, I was shy and tender with women. Giselle said that the French had held out a dream coat for me and I had snuggled into it and made it my own. She liked to tear it to tatters and snigger at what she found beneath.

I hung around in cafés because I didn't have much to do. The students in Censier were on strike for the third time that term and nobody turned up for my Composition and Comprehension class. I was sick to the teeth of playing Martin Luther King's 'I have a Dream' speech and asking the students to summarise it in a third of its length. We had Martin Luther King on tape to show how progressive and radical we were compared with the Law Faculty. Periodically, the law students would descend on Censier, smash the place up with iron bars and light fires in the lecture halls. The more the merrier, as far as I was concerned. The break for revolution freed me from having to change my shirt, comb my hair or invest in deodorants. I cultivated the wild look.

It was a good life. I never got up before eleven. By that time the world was fully inflated, the streets aired and people had lost the bitter taste of their dreams. In the language laboratory I chatted up the girls in the booths instead of correcting their English pronunciation. Every evening I drank myself into the ground. I did it in order to keep myself from sleepwalking. In Galway I was often half way to the docks before my mother caught me.

'You are a pest to yourself', said Giselle lighting a cigarette in my narrow bed in the Franco-Brittanique. 'All the clichés about the Irish are true.'

She always turned vicious when she felt secure and gratified.

'Then why did you come to bed with me?'

'Because I thought you were a Gaelic peasant. Or a poet. But I was wrong. You are very average. If you were a Patrick Kavanagh or someone like that I would have the reason to support your lack of finesse. But you are sentimental. *Vulgaire.*'

She stubbed out her cigarette in my shoe and hoisted her honey odalisque body from the bed.

'Besides, I would never think of living with a man who cannot learn French. There must be a blockage in you. Shit. *Je déteste les petits lits.*'

'What's that?' I asked.

So I was a pest to myself. What did she mean? In Galway I was famous for my imagination. It was in the blood. When I was fifteen my poems were published in *The Clare Champion* under a girl's name in case my mother found out. I knew I was a poet, even if I had stopped writing. I had to stop because every poem cost me a breakdown. I couldn't handle the exaltation. It blew my fuses. I had the courage to shut up. I was like an oyster with a pearl stuck in my gut. I savoured my oysterishness, the hard shell and the briny succulence within. Giselle wanted to shuck me open and display the nacre of my irritants. Why couldn't she take me just as I was? But then, I had to admit she had a point. Why did I grow a beard and wear a long black coat and granny glasses? Why did I put 'writer' in my passport? Why did I quote Joyce about silence, exile and cunning? More and more, I felt a nauseating obligation to be what I always wanted to be.

It was nauseating but unavoidable. Between my finger and my thumb the pen pointed, sharp as a hypodermic syringe. If nothing else, poetry would be my pest control.

I thought I should begin from erotica the way painters begin from the nude. I strode the paths of the Luxembourg Gardens like a rhapsodic whore, giving myself to every naked statue I met. Leda, Aphrodite, Galatea, Pan, Apollo, Demeter. God or Goddess, I tried them all. I whispered shameless words to them. I was unfaithful. I loved them and left them and took what I could from them. I rummaged through encyclopaedias and dictionaries for names, legends, previous liaisons. I craved their stories, as intimate as possible, to possess them more completely. *Galatea: one of the nereids, beautiful maidens, reputedly benevolent, though there is some doubt among scholars on this point; in short, rather ill-defined creatures. Galatea was the lover of the gentle shepherd, Acis, and was raped by the Cyclops, Polyphemus.*

I watched the three of them at the Fontaine de Medici. Galatea arching her body delightedly in the lap of Acis. Cool long white limbs in a dripping grotto. An erotic pietà. They gaze at one another in wonder, unaware of the dark shadow falling from above. An immense one-eyed Cyclops watches them, black with rage and jealousy. *The Cyclopes were gross and ill-mannered, they bred in isolated caves and slaughtered and devoured strangers.*

Polyphemus holds the rock that will crush Acis and leave

Galatea at his mercy. His hand, clumsy by her hand, the fingers bunched to hide snagged dirty nails, a scorpion scrofulous on a cyclamen. The lips flaccid, held close over a mouth gapped by the bit of lust and years. Odour of turds, sour curds and whey.

Again and again I returned to Polyphemus. I did not care for the lovers. Him I understood. I recalled sheep in the kitchen, piss in the hand basin, belches and farts, no matter the occasion. I saw his eye reddened by turf smoke, his hair matted by wind and rain, a rim of Galatea's blood round his lips. His roguish glance denied any hand act or part in the crime. He had the acid smell of a man who had never been loved.

The title of my first (and only) collection of poems was *O'Sullivan in the Luxembourg Gardens*. It was weird. The verses almost wrote themselves. As I took them down in the Franco-Brittanique I could sense the Cyclops in the room, acrid and unhappy. I wrapped his lechery in an expensive black leather cover and had the verses printed in thick Gothic type. The book was issued privately in a limited signed edition of five copies.

The first copy, after much hesitation, I sent to mother. The second went as a belated wedding present to Kate, my twin sister. The third I sent to our national poet, A.T. Harrington. The fourth I slipped under Giselle's pillow. The fifth I kept for myself.

And the gates of Hell opened. The first sign of trouble was a letter from the brother-in-law in Ballyvaughan.

'I'll never forgive you for what you've done,' wrote P.J.

'You've destroyed your sister, and you've picked the right time to do it.'

It turned out that shortly after the birth of her first child, Kate read the poems and went out of her poor mind. She said worms and snakes were coming out of the book. She tried to exorcise them with salt and holy water but the things only grew bigger and fatter. She asked P.J. to put the book away in the attic, but the snakes came twirling down the cord of the electric light and dropped on the baby's cradle. So P.J. went to Father Boniface in the Friary in Athlone for help. Father Boniface told them to find a large full-grown oak tree and bury the book beneath it. That way the evil power would be absorbed and neutralised. They had the devil's own job to find an oak tree in Clare. But they did as the holy priest told them and the snakes disappeared. How dare I send them such an evil thing?

P.J. demanded that I leave my sister alone and send her no more books. Paris was obviously the place for the likes of me.

Giselle loved the book until she read it. When I met her after her concert in the Sacré Coeur she was cool and withdrawn. She sang in the choir and I had to go to her weekend concerts if I wanted to sleep with her.

'Is anything the matter?' I asked.

'It's your problem, not mine.'

I felt an icy draft. 'You didn't like my poems, then?'

'I could certainly do without the dedication.'

We walked in the brittle silence I knew all too well to the door of her apartment.

'If you come in,' she said, 'you will sleep on the couch.'

At least she hadn't left me out on the street.

Giselle's favourite colour was white. Everything in the sitting room – the pillows on the couch, the lampshades, the carpet, the TV cabinet, the bookcases, the budgerigar's cage – was white. She had a white desk in her white bedroom where she sat for ten hours a day preparing for her Agrégation.

The righteous innocence of the interior seemed to magnify the offence I had committed. I tried to take Giselle's hand but she didn't want to be touched.

'It's not that easy,' she said. 'I don't want to be wanted in that way. You need another kind of woman. Go to Pigalle and queue up with the Arabs.'

'But don't be so damn silly, Giselle. The man who creates and the man who loves are not the same. You know that.'

'*Mon Dieu*, what big words! Well, if that's the case, both your love and your creation are in a bad taste. Very bad taste, do you understand? But for me, I don't care a pin.'

She moved towards the bedroom.

'I have much to do for tomorrow. Please turn the lights off when you finish.'

I realised then how bad it was. I had been helping her with her preparation for the Agrégation. Either she had found somebody else or she despised the ground I walked on. The key turned in her bedroom door.

'Fuck you! I'm not going to rape you!'

Dear God, but I wanted to. I thought of her in her short chemise, lying on her belly in her chaste brass bed and I would have given anything just to touch the nape of her neck.

There were two bottles of pink champagne on the sideboard. Giselle used to fantasise about drinking champagne after making love. I kept forgetting to bring her a bottle. I thought: I might just as well have a drink now that I'm here. I managed to stain the couch and the carpet a bit. Then I opened the second bottle and I thought: I might just as well spoil it entirely now that I'm here. But even the champagne didn't quench the pain of loss that raged in my bowels.

The room bristled with contempt. The more I drank the more it rejected me. I could feel the irritation in the carpet and the couch's malaise under me. I couldn't bear the white blizzard any more.

I walked back to the Cité-Universitaire, all twenty kilometres of the way. I had forgotten to take my jacket and there was a cold wind blowing. It swept across the steppes of Russia, over the Tatra Mountains, down the ice-clad valleys of the Alps and pin-pointed me on the Rue Mouftard, where I knew for sure that I was a sick man.

First thing in the morning I rang Giselle to get back my jacket and the book. Reluctantly she agreed to meet me at the Hôtel de Ville. I was wet with fever and a bit delirious and barely able to clamber up the steps of the metro. She was crossing Pont Neuf when I spotted her – long-legged Giselle with the chestnut page boy hair and jasmine face. Would she have me back? Would she take pity on my broken body?

'You left the lights on and destroyed the carpet. Would you at least replace the champagne you stole?' Giselle was up on her high horse.

'No, I won't.'

'Very well,' she said, 'I didn't think you could stoop so low.'

'Giselle,' I begged in a voice strangled by catarrh and grief, 'I'm not like that at all. I'll change. Cross my heart.'

'*Pas du tout*. You never change. You make all these elaborate plans and projects, but it's all in your head, do you understand? I don't think you can evolve at all. Why did you write this . . . this . . . ?'

I was just about to explain everything when something possessed me, a phrase I don't know from where.

'Hook'em Horns,' I said, half to myself.

'What?'

'Hook'em Horns!' I repeated aloud and held up my fist with the index and the little fingers extended.

'What are you doing? Stop it at once! Are you mad?'

I jabbed my fingers at her face.

'Hook'em Horns!'

She looked at me in fear.

'Hook'em Horns!' I cried ever more joyously. She began to run. I followed her. Still running, she opened her shoulder bag and took out a parcel.

'Hook'em Horns!'

Next thing I saw was my book in the air being pursued by a squawking gull. When I looked over the parapet of the bridge it had disappeared into the thick waters of the Seine.

Like the good little Catholic French bourgeois bitch she

was, she posted me my jacket which arrived the next day. There was also a note from Censier to let me know that classes had resumed.

On my way to the Language Laboratory I collapsed. I woke up in a clean white room. At first I thought I was at Giselle's and turned over in the bed to touch her. Then I found that there was another bed in the room with a young man asleep in it. My brain was clenching and unclenching and my chest was hooped with an iron bar. Suddenly I felt my brain sliding down the inside of my left nostril. When I blew my nose it fell out in a bloody clot on the sheet. I knew I had to get it back inside so I grabbed the lump and swallowed it quickly. After recovering my brain I went back to sleep again. When I woke the next time I saw a nurse astride the young man in the other bed, her white uniform pulled up round her thighs. Slowly, they made love in the soft glow of the night lamp.

I had viral pneumonia. I was bursting with joy. At last I could stay in bed, cloud-drifting all day long. When my temperature fell I spent days and nights reading *The Brothers Karamazov*. Father Zossima's sermon on love made me cry. Night after night I lay there weeping happily while my room mate and the nurse mated in the next bed.

It was a joyous, enchanted time for the three of us. Sometimes, as she rode him, the nurse would glance at me with demure affection and I would smile back through my Russian tears. In the fervid dawns after she had left, I wrote letters to everybody I knew, begging for forgiveness and quoting long passages from Dostoevsky.

I never spoke to my room-mate, but like everybody else I couldn't take my eyes off him. I christened him Endymion because of his sleepy, beautiful face. He slept during the day except when he had visitors. Most were not allowed to see him and just waved through the glass top of the door. I waved back for him. By evening his bed would be surrounded with bouquets of flowers. Somehow I learned, I don't know how, that he was dying of spinal cancer.

My mother arrived on the day I was discharged from hospital. She came to Paris equipped with her electric geyser. We sat in her hotel room and drank cup after cup of Lyons Green Label tea. She talked about the neighbours at home. They were dying like flies. She had been in France many times on pilgrimages to Lourdes but never got as far as Paris before. Apart from visiting me she wanted to see the miraculously preserved body of St Thérèse in the Rue de Bac. But what had I been up to? If I said my prayers and led a regular life and wore warm underwear none of this would have happened. She was so pleased at my recovery that she broke the pledge and drank a bottle of wine with me at Le Dôme.

'Now,' she said, 'take me to the Luxembourg Gardens and show me the Thing.'

The pigeons were sousing their feathers in the brimming water of the fountain. A string quartet played 'The Four Seasons' in the gazebo nearby. Mother sat looking at the statues for a long time.

'What do you think of yer man?' I asked with deliberate casualness and pointed up to Polyphemus on his rocky ledge above the lovers. He was the only one of the three with his clothes on.

'To tell you the truth not a great deal,' she replied. 'I expected a lot worse.'

Both of us were somehow disappointed.

'So you don't see anything in it?'

'It's all made up, isn't it? Giants and nymphs and all that. Unreal.'

'And my book,' I said, louder than necessary. 'What did you do with my book?'

Her face hardened.

'Malachi, Malachi. It was the same with your father.'

She had a habit of making enigmatic remarks about my father without further explanation. Long ago I understood that whatever was on her mind was so terrible that I simply couldn't face it. So I had given up asking.

'What did you do with my book? You burnt it, didn't you?'

'So I did,' she replied calmly.

'You always burn my stuff! Even when I was little. And all I wanted to do was to express my feelings and put things straight.'

I was angry with myself because I could feel the tears coming.

'Keep your feelings to yourself the same as the rest of us. And pray God to forgive you for your idolatry.'

'What do you mean?'

'You called the wolf from the forest with that book of yours,' she said solemnly. 'If you have any more copies, get rid of them.'

Before she left for Ireland she gave me a rosary that had been blessed by Father Peyton at Knock.

The final nail in the coffin of *O'Sullivan* was a letter I found in my box when I returned to the Collège Franco-Brittanique. It was written by a friend of A.T. Harrington's in Santa Monica. He was sorry to inform me that the great poet had died in unexplained circumstances. There would be a commemorative mass in a side chapel of St Patrick's Cathedral in New York and a meal for his friends in a Hawaiian restaurant in Greenwich Village. I was invited to attend both and to contribute to a commemorative volume of poems and essays.

For a moment I was shot through with a sense of tremendous power. My words could blight or maim or kill! I knew what the Druids of ancient Ireland knew when they rhymed rats to death.

I needed to touch my totem again. It was odd. *O'Sullivan* seemed perfectly innocuous. A bit extravagant on the outside, perhaps, but inside it was like any other sequence of poems. What was wrong? What was all the hullabaloo about? I leafed back and forth through the pages in bewilderment.

Just then, as I glanced at my hand on the page, I saw that it trembled uncontrollably. It seemed cut off from the rest of me and to be frightened all by itself. Then the fear began to spread, to my throat, to my belly, to my knees. I was trembling all over. What was it? Why was I shaking like this? Was it a relapse?

He was in the room with me, beseeching, greedy for affection in the way I had always known him. He winked roguishly, as if nothing had happened, as if the terrible thing had never been done. Like mother, I averted my eyes. Like her I said Jesus, Mary and Joseph, Help me. I saw my hands dismembering the book, page after page until the floor was littered with tiny pieces of paper. Only the leather cover remained, the skin of a flayed beast.

I, Liam O'Sullivan, the one-eyed, saved humanity from myself.

Béal dúnta agus súile oscailte.

My Last Chance

Let me tell you how I found myself in the Swami Majundar Chattopadhayaya's shoes.

Like all the odd and disastrous happenings in my life over the last while, it had a connection with my friend Bernard Slattery. One morning in early September, Bernard stood in the door of my office with a look of docile contentment on his face.

'I pulled through the last bout,' he sighed and collapsed into the armchair.

I envied him. He sprawled there emptied of his frenzy in a crisp shirt and cravat with his smarmy eyes focused on my stained pullover.

'Was it bad?' I asked, hoping to push him back into it at least for a moment so that he wouldn't be so smug.

'Not really,' he grimaced. 'I enjoyed the elation bit. Up there you think you can do anything. Write four books at a time. Learn Polish. Anything.'

'But then?'

'Yes.'

'Go on.'

But he only smiled helplessly and raised his pudgy hand in an aimless wave.

'How's Kim keeping?' he asked.

I felt my hand repeating his gesture. I wondered why he asked me about her. He had never asked about my wife before.

Two days later he sent me a letter from Dublin. It contained the programme for the 'Swami Majundar's Intensive' to be held in two months time. 'The Swami is a Living Hindu Saint,' the programme said. 'Two and a half days of intimate and personal association with a living saint will be an experience that will uplift and transform your soul *forever*.'

Slattery had underlined the word 'forever' several times in red ink and had written on the margin: '*Your last chance!!!*'

That same day it so happened that I was reading the Master Peter Duinov's *Spiritual Galvanoplasty*. Five minutes in the company of a sage or a saint was worth more than twenty years in a University, said Duinov.

That was it. First Slattery and then Duinov. *Nomen omen*, in short.

For years I have been dreaming that one day a sage or a saint would touch me on the forehead with his index finger and ZAP I would be enlightened and the pains in my head would vanish on the spot. Even now, when I think about this, I can, for a moment, feel what that instant would be like. It would be like the shock of clarity and excitement that I felt as a child when my mother washed my hair and I had to tip back my head and she poured cold, cold water to rinse it out.

It distressed me that Slattery had underlined the word

'forever' and added '*Your last chance*' in red ink. I got a whiff of hysteria off that. But I knew what he was getting at. He was getting at my four misfortunes.

(1) My wife

My wife left me because I got middle-aged, ugly and read the *Masters of the Great White Lodge* day and night. Just after she bailed out, I started visiting churches and chapels, Catholic or Protestant, it didn't matter a damn. I tried to blackmail God into doing something about my case. But all the time I knew that He had me cornered because I didn't go to mass on Sundays. That's where the real action is.

(2) My father

My father is dying of senile dementia, same as Churchill. He's mad as a brush and thinks I'm his favourite uncle. I remember once, when I was a boy, he pointed to his own father and said: 'Take a good look at your grandfather. Mad as a hatter. I'll be like that. And so will you.'

(3) My sons

My sons should love me because I'm their father. But they don't. If they write to me now and then it's because they want money for a computer. All their friends have computers.

(4) My sneeze

There is one almighty sneeze in me that comes out in drips and drabs. Since my childhood I've suffered from attacks of sneezing as soon as I get up in the morning.

Must be some sort of allergy to life. Like my cousin Father Sean who was attacked by a poltergeist in Africa, I'm in mortal fear of thinking about anything for the first three hours of the day. If I start thinking I start sneezing. Out of bed, shower (if I'm not too fragile), breakfast, *The Irish Times*, off to work and not a thought in my head. I switch on my mind when I pass the first chestnut tree on the avenue into college.

I don't have a car any more – the wife took the lot – so I went to the Swami by bus. When I got to Donnybrook I realised that I hadn't the faintest notion where the session was to be held. And there wasn't much point in asking your average Dubliner where the Swami Majundar was hanging out. But when the pupil is ready the master appears – or at least one of his disciples. I saw this chap walking towards me in the rain and recognised him from the old days in Transcendental Meditation. I could not, and still cannot for the life of me, remember his name except that he was English and that I used to call him Sidhaman. The sidhis are special powers developed by meditation and yoga such as flying, invisibility, passing through walls and such like. He was a Sidha.

I hadn't seen him for years but I noticed something I had noticed before: he had begun to look distinctly oriental. I've seen this happen to others who have meditated for a long time. The oriental quality has nothing to do with developing slant eyes or anything like that. It's more a subtle aura and expresses itself most visibly in a cheerful, cherubic face and in the hair which grows bushy, luxurious and guru-like. I've seen the same sort of convergence among pig dealers in Cavan. They become like their pigs right down to growing white bristles on their wet noses.

When we approached the gates of Shanti Cottage I saw Slattery. I was thunderstruck. He seemed punctured. His jaw was hacked with razor cuts and the shreds of newspaper he had used to dry the blood still stuck to it. He endlessly corrected the angle of his glasses. The eyes were big and frantic as damsons. There was still some cheer in him though because we embraced on meeting as usual. He is the only man I ever embrace in this way.

I asked him what in the name of Jasus had happened to him. He told me he had cracked up. Too much sex. He seemed reluctant to say any more so I left it at that. As usual he was dressed very elegantly in a tight three-piece pinstripe suit with a Harvard tie and a scarlet rose in his buttonhole.

As the senior man present I knocked on the door of Shanti Cottage. A slim girl in saffron robes and yellow socks beckoned us in. She had long brown hair and a bright red mark on her forehead. She spoke with a hacked South African accent which got between me and everything she said.

She asked us to take off our shoes. Thank God I had clean socks on. We were shown into the sitting room, the usual sort of building estate sitting room. Except that there were yellow flowers everywhere, daffodils, primroses and mimosa to match her yellow saffron robes. Yellow, gold, saffron are the colours of enlightenment. I know the ropes.

There were mattresses on the floor. Anybody who has done the TM-Sidhi Programme knows exactly what they're for. When you do the flying sutra you rise up in the air and come crashing down very hard on the arse. But here the mattresses were being used by the lapsed Sidhas for sitting on. In the bay window there was a large couch covered with a clean white sheet and beside the couch a little altar with a picture of Krishna and his wife. I forget her name.

Krishna's face was blue, his wife's was white. It made a change from fiery Sacred Hearts and bleeding crucifixes. Here were two lovers, a god with his bride leaning on his shoulder. I was excited by the picture of this happy couple.

'Cool it,' said Slattery. 'It's not what you think. The girl is really Krishna's soul.'

I had a problem. I had bought *The Irish Times* at the bus station. Would it be sacrilegious to read it in the yellow room while waiting for the Swami? I decided that it was OK. I was encouraged in this decision by two newly arrived devotees. They were discussing what the Swami taught about sainthood. He had said that a saint was an ordinary man doing ordinary things. So I decided that it was all right to read *The Irish Times*. But I must admit that I felt very uncomfortable and put it down several times just in case. It seemed a profane sort of thing to be doing.

I happened to be reading when the Swami came into the room for a moment to check the sound level on the tape recorder hidden under the couch. As a mark of respect I hastily stood up. All the others, more versed in oriental custom, bowed their heads to the floor. I felt confused and so did the Swami. He too was dressed in saffron robes and yellow stockings. He had a magnificent, leonine head with a great broad brow. He did not speak to me. Instead, he chatted away to the others about the rain and Macintosh computers. Then he bounded out again.

People were exchanging confidences about the Swami. There were a number of devotees travelling round the world with him. One was a middle-aged Danish-German-Californian lady dressed in ordinary clothes. Clearly she was not as far advanced along the path as the girl in saffron. I learned from her that the Swamiji ('ji' is diminutive and expresses affection: thus 'Little Swami') was famous for not answering questions. One person would ask him a question one day and the Swami would refuse to answer. Another person would ask the same question the next day and the Swami would reply at great length. It all depended on your purity of heart. The American lady told me that Swamiji had answered all her questions every time at extraordinary length and would even say: 'Are you sure you understand now, Ruthie? You are sure?' and she inclined her head in imitation of the Swami.

I knew the type. Teacher's pet. God forgive me, I wondered to myself if she had money and if the Swami was sleeping with the South African girl. I'm convinced this evil thought was the start of my troubles.

While we were all sitting quietly waiting for the Swami the girl in saffron hovered around us like a brimstone butterfly. I couldn't help musing on how far she had to carry this saffron clothes thing. Were her knickers saffron, for example? I began to sweat.

Slattery and Sidhaman were in the middle of the room. Suddenly Sidhaman got up, mumbled an apology and went to sit right up beside the couch. I was furious.

This was the kind of impudence that gained the Brits an Empire. Then, to my surprise, the saffron girl, as if reading my thoughts, asked me if I would like to sit up beside the Master. I ended up even closer to the couch than Sidhaman and I could see the hostility in his eyes. It was all, as I afterwards realised, done with a purpose.

The Swami appeared. The sanyassins prostrated themselves with extraordinary alacrity and joy. Swami sat cross–legged on the couch. I noticed that he had strong muscular arms and a very expensive Swiss golden watch on his wrist. He intoned a Sanskrit chant. He was a different man from the one who had chatted about the weather and Macintosh computers. It was as if the chant separated him from all profanity. His eyes did not seem to be looking anywhere. He spoke of attachment and ambition as the cords that bind us to the world.

He had a cold. He blew huge quantities of snot into, not a handkerchief, but a large yellow towel. I think I began to lose my faith in him when I saw that he had a cold. At the end of the talk he asked were there any questions. There was silence.

'Very, very good,' he said. 'Questions are a sign of a disturbed mind. They are asked by the uncentred person.'

There was a long pause. The Swami chanted another holy verse and came down to earth. The formalities were over.

Sidhaman had just became a father. Wasn't it wonderful? Swami giggled with delight. The South African girl giggled too and asked Swami who loves a child most, the mother or the father? Swami looked at her tenderly. She shone back at him. A wave of joy rippled between them.

The Swami said: 'Once upon a time and a long time ago when turkeys chewed tobacco and birds built their nests in old men's beards, there was a poor village in India. Two women called on a wise old headman with a new-born child. "It's my son!" said one. "Liar!" said the other. "He's mine. Judge between us, O wise one." The headman thought for seven days and seven nights and then called the women to him. "Since you cannot agree," he said, "I'll take this sword and carve the child in two. Each of you will have one half of the boy. Justice will be done." "Very, very good," said one of the women. "No!" cried the other one. "Spare the boy! I give up my claim to him!" And that was how the headman knew that she was the true mother and gave the child back to her.'

I can tell you I was upset. Here was this Indian creature telling an Indian story that I damn well knew from the Old Testament. More, it had nothing to do with the question that had been asked, as far as I could see. I glanced at Slattery who was hanging on Swami's every word with a look that said, what a genius this man is! What culture! What insight!

'It's Solomon,' I said. 'Solomon, for Christ's sake.'

'Hang loose,' he replied. 'Solomon got it from the Indians.'

We were interrupted by Ruth who decided that it was time to introduce me to the Swami. She addressed me as Professor. A Professor! Among all the unemployed, the disabled and the neurotic that filled the room there was a Professor! I was a prize offering to the Swami.

'A professor of what?' he asked, unimpressed.

'I'm not a professor,' I said. 'I lecture in biochemistry.'

'Very, very good,' he replied. Chemistry is important.

I'd very much like to discuss the Bloom Hamilton reaction later on.'

He scared me.

Lunch was a vegetarian concoction that caused me to break large quantities of wind. I found it extremely embarrassing. Then Slattery insisted that I join him for a drink. He wanted to tell me about his breakdown.

For the last years I've been hearing about breakdowns, causing breakdowns, enduring breakdowns, handling breakdowns. I know the scenario inside out and the ritual of its telling. We would go to a pub, we would drink pints of porter, we would chain smoke and talk man to man. The only variation in Slattery's story had to do with his girl. She regularly mugged him whenever he threatened to leave her. She also bit him savagely on the thighs. He had to wear long johns all summer to conceal the welts from his wife.

So I sat in the pub listening to Slattery's confession and festering with guilt. This time it wasn't the wife or my sons or my dereliction that were worrying me but the Swami. He had instructed us to remain centred and on no account to move outside the orbit of harmony.

After four pints we returned to the house for the afternoon session. Swami was absent. He was up in his room performing private devotions. So Ruthie led us through Interpersonal Relaxation. We were asked to talk about our experiences, what everybody actually felt. Most of the discussion was taken up by the devotees describing how they had met the Swami. The girl in yellow knickers described how she met the Swamiji while hitch-hiking in Uttar Pradesh. Slattery described how he had heard about Swami from Luke O'Brady. Sidhaman ditto. One after another they all described how they had met the Swami. He had come just when they needed him as the fulfilment of their desires.

'I'm very very sure that I met him in an earlier incarnation,' said Ruthie. 'Swami told me that I would not be able to stand his presence for more than a few minutes if we had not worked together in a previous life.'

'It's amazing, really,' chimed in another American lady. 'Folks back home run from Swamiji's lectures in terror. Once we were in this home for retired Jewish executives in Pasadena. The Intensive began with three hundred and fifty people and ended with, like, five.'

'Ireland is truly a wonderfully spiritual country,' broke in Ruthie. 'Just think. Nobody but nobody has left a single one of the Swami's meetings here in Dublin. It's the rosary, I'm sure. It's the long, long devotional tradition in your country.'

Sidhaman nodded his head.

'You either run towards the Swami or you run away from him. Look at me. I'm falling over a cliff into his arms.'

His voice had taken on a faint American twang.

A refined alto whetted, by too many whiskies and Dunhills confessed: 'A year or so ago if I didn't have a man at night I'd chew the bloody wallpaper. But now there's such peace . . . such peace . . . '

Her voice broke and she sobbed. She was still wearing a black leather skirt with zebra tights, but I suppose she must have changed inside.

The atmosphere in the sitting room was balsamic and suffused with loving acceptance. You could say whatever you wanted. When it came to my turn I said that, quite honestly, I felt like running away. Ruth tried to look at me with pity but it came out as reproach. She shook her head and folded her arms à la Swami.

'It's your ego. You can't drop your ego, can you? Just because you've been so successful in life your ego can't let it go.'

Then we had a session of chanting to purify the atmosphere. It was led by the South African girl. She gave each of us a sheet with Sanskrit phrases and a translation underneath. She chanted the phrases first, then we followed. They were all about the loving looks which passed between Krishna and his bride as described by the Gopis. They were supposed to be very powerful.

I could not take part. Firstly, I sing out of tune. Secondly, I was beginning to feel very sick. I had a pain in my head and, to my horror, I was passing wind at a fearsome rate. To this day I don't know if it was the vegetarian food, the Guinness or the power of the purifying chant that caused it.

When the Swami came down for his evening talk I started sneezing as well. Just as he began I had to lie down on the floor. This was my third misfortune. Earlier we had been told that it was a mark of great disrespect to a Holy Man to point one's feet at him. So there I was, sick as a dog, farting like a trooper, sneezing like a Turk and lying on the floor with my feet pointing at the Swami while he went on and on about the reasons why Krishna had a blue face.

I couldn't hold it in any longer. I just had to leave. Trembling and farting vigorously I got up on my hunkers. Swami paused. I looked around in despair. It was impossible to get out without trampling over everybody. I could feel the sanyassins willing me out of the room. Their eyes stuck to me like leeches. I forced myself to clamber over arms and legs. To make things worse, one of the devotees was fast asleep against the door. I shook him gently by the shoulder, but he wouldn't budge. Then I kicked him. He opened his sleepy eyes for a moment and muttered 'Go fuck yourself.'

The horror of that blasphemy in the Holy Man's presence spread like a stain round the room. I tried to haul him away from the door but I simply couldn't. He was too heavy and inert. The devotees gazed impassively at my efforts. I began to sneeze again, the panic tightening in my chest. That's where it hits me.

Then I heard an anchor chain rattling out of a ship's bows. It was the Swami blowing his nose. The next moment he leapt from the divan, clambered over his followers who yearned to be touched by him, picked up the sleeping man like a cat and lugged him across the room to the couch where he dumped him, still sound asleep. I stood there, stunned. Swami looked at me sadly and pointed to the door with his chin.

Outside in the street it was pouring rain. I felt forsaken and exiled. I had a sudden urge to run back, throw myself into Swami's arms and cry, 'Swamiji, take me!'

My feet were sogging wet. I had forgotten to put on my shoes. They were stuck somewhere at the back of the meditation room. Hopelessness welled up in me again. Kim's voice exulted: Idiot! It won't be long now!

Just then I heard two plops behind me and the sound of a window being firmly closed. On the pavement were a pair of large brown Indian sandals. When I poked my feet into them I found that they were at least four sizes too large. I was about to put them back through the letter-box when it dawned on me how truly honoured I was. Those others in the room there would have given anything for a touch, a smile, a nod from the Swami. And I – I had the Master's sandals!

I put them on with reverence, stuffing my socks into the heels so that they wouldn't flip-flop too much. Bashfully I strode to the bus stop, while from aerials and tree tops, hedges and hoardings, sleek-winged and astonished, the magpies jeered me on.

Beatha dhuine a thoil.

An Unusual Couple

When we phoned Jack and Tracey for the umpteenth time that summer and nobody answered we knew that they were both dead. The phone rang and rang into vacancy. Nobody descended the polished oak staircase or climbed up from the beef-smelling bowels of the kitchen. The glassy eye of the stag's head glared down on the panelled hallway, on the rack of fishing rods, and on the monster trout from Lough Derrylea. We could see it as if we were there.

Last time Tracey was in Galway she went to her solicitor and made a will. Afterwards, she dropped in for a cup of tea and told us that she had left us her lovely Pleiade edition of the French classics and the big new motor-powered lawnmower. As usual we were furious with her. She was filthy rich and instead of inviting us out for a big meal or a cocktail before her demise she came to us for a measly cup of tea.

She said that basically she wasn't interested in going on. Jack wasn't interested either. The only thing that was keeping them together was the dogs. Derrylea House needed to be refurbished but they just didn't have the zing for it any more. We suggested that maybe she should buy a video and lots of tapes for the winter to cheer things up a bit. But all that was beneath her. She wanted something more fulfilling. She didn't know what. Perhaps French poetry. Or herbal medicine. Or sailing. Or dying. It was all the same anyhow. As for Jack, he preferred to sleep.

The last weekend in July we decided to go and view the bodies. The way to Derrylea House took us through the snottiest countryside in the West of Ireland. As usual the rain lashed the bedraggled hitch-hikers that perched all along the road.

'We're going to give lifts to the dregs,' said Hugo, ignoring two Scandinavian blondes with a placard reading CLIFTON PLEASE. 'Smelly old men. Old women with plastic shopping bags and no teeth. Hairy dwarfs and mongols.'

'OK, I'll choose,' I said.

Connemara was all inky and runny. Sloppy clouds dragged their skirts over the hills. Boy, were we glad that we had spent four weeks in Antiparos. Tracey, of course, used to go to France in search of The Meaning of Life. On one of her expeditions she met Jack at a St Patrick's Day party in the Irish Embassy. He was over in Paris trying to flog Galway Bay oysters and mussels to the French. He looked drawn and yellow, like a corrupt double agent from Casablanca. He had all the allure of a man who was to be shot at dawn. Tracey looked like the kind of woman who could painlessly inherit his money. They fitted well together. Or that's how we imagined it from Tracey's morbid tales over tea.

They settled down in Connemara in an old dower house beside a lake. They had six dogs together, two cocker spaniels and four labradors.

'Those damn dogs,' said Hugo. 'I hope Jack has them tied up this time.'

'Maybe they did away with the dogs as well?'

'And the housekeeper! What do you call her? The one with the moustache. A real funeral pyre!' Hugo slowed down. 'And now, would you cast your eye over that creature on the side of the road.'

The creature was loping along, no jacket, shirt open, a pair of red braces holding up baggy trousers. Big muddy boots. It was the way I had always imagined Christy Mahon.

'Good Lord, but won't you get a flu?' asked Hugo opening the back door.

'If the flu saw me it would run away,' replied Christy Mahon, getting into the car. He stank of Guinness and stale socks. He had been on his way to Galway to look for work. He had stood in the rain for two hours, but nobody gave him a lift so he was walking back to Carna.

'What kind of work are you after?' asked Hugo.

'Digging ditches. Road mending. Anything with a pick and shovel. I'm told there's a power of work going in Galway.'

There was a dark bruise on his face and scabs on the back of his hands. It was because he walked into things when he had a few jars, he explained. He was on the dole and had £10 left over for drink every week. But people were good to him and he often drank five times that amount.

'Are you happy in yourself?' asked Hugo.

It was an unusual question to ask a stranger. But then, we are an unusual couple.

'It's like this,' he said. 'A man can only sleep so much, drink so much and eat so much. I sleep and I eat and I drink as much as the next man. Why wouldn't I be happy?'

'But aren't you envious of people with cars and houses and families?'

'Not wan bit. As long as a man has enough to eat and drink and a place to sleep, what more would he want?'

We drove happily through the rain, cheered by his folk wisdom. Before Carna, Hugo made one last effort to squeeze some more of it out of him.

'Do you believe in God?'

The man thought carefully for a minute.

'I do and I don't.'

'Well, do you pray for example?'

'I only pray in the winter. I say to God, God, I don't understand you. Maybe you don't understand me either. But take me home with you when I die. Amen.'

He had brought himself to the verge of tears. He leaned over the back seat.

'Can you lend me the loan of a tenner? I won't insult you by asking for less.'

'I can't give you ten quid, I'm afraid,' said Hugo. 'But there's an old raincoat in the boot. You can have it if you want.'

Christy Mahon's head jerked forward angrily.

'A coat is it? Who the fuck do you think I am? A tinker? Let me out of this fucking jalopy. Stick your fucking raincoat and your questions up your arse!'

When he got out of the car he kicked the back bumper a few times.

'The poor have only words with which to defend themselves,' said Hugo putting on a tape.

'And there are enough words in this country to fill all the mouths,' I added.

We both laughed. A Mozart sonata cleansed the air of what was left of Christy Mahon.

'I wonder if they shot themselves or hanged themselves,' mused Hugo. 'Remember the man they found in the stables in Tuam?'

'Never heard.'

'Swinging from a rope. Right beside him there was another halter with a note pinned to it for the wife: "Brigit, this is for you".'

Not Tracey's or Jack's style, I thought. More likely an overdose or the car exhaust. Nothing very energetic, anyway. Jack was chronically tired and did everything half way. He hardly dressed himself properly any more and wore his pyjama top as a shirt. Sometimes he stopped shaving half way. 'What's the use for Christ's sake?' he would ask, and go back to bed. Then Tracey would descend on us in despair and we would analyse Jack for hours and hours. At every visit we learned that he had stopped doing this or that. It was as if some great rickety machine was closing down one engine after another and gradually shuddering to a dead stop.

At first Tracey spent her days planning how to escape Jack and Derrylea House. She would put the dogs down and go to Martinique. She would start up an antique furniture shop on the docks in Galway. She would invite the vet for dinner and see what happened.

But she never did anything. She hounded us to death for ideas of what she might do or whom she might seduce or where she should go with all her money and her good looks. She was deeply interested in getting interested in something, something broadening for example. She booked an adventure holiday to Kenya, got all the books, the mosquito net and the injections. At the last minute she turned back at Dublin Airport. She told us that when she had talked about things long enough she felt so relieved that she didn't have to do them any more.

She read most of the day. The rest of the time she walked the dogs, smoked pot and waited for something to happen. Nothing happened. In the spring she and Jack began to argue a lot about death before going to bed. Their exchanges were icy and dispassionate, as if they were discussing the forthcoming visit of some elderly, unwelcome relative.

'Speaking about unwelcome visitors,' said Hugo, 'what about this one?'

He stopped the car a few yards ahead of a woman hitch-hiker.

'You're so kind, so kind,' she said as she bundled herself into the car. 'And I'm so wet.'

She spoke with a slight foreign accent. I thought she looked like a forty-year-old superannuated hippie. She wore black tights with jazzy woollen knee-socks up to the hemline of her leather mini-skirt. Her face was tired and pinched, as if her skin was too tightly stretched over the bones.

'Bad cess to it but it's very bad weather for the ould arthritis,' she said in an idiom borrowed from some local sufferer.

'Where do you live?' asked Hugo.

'In a caravan a few miles down the road. That's where I got the pains in me hands and neck. Are you from Galway?'

'Yes, ' we replied together. 'And you?'

'Holland,' she confessed guiltily, as if being from Holland was a crime. 'But I was in Galway for the last two days to buy a book,' she added quickly. 'You see, I want a house. I can't live any more in the caravan. The pains are killing me.'

'What's the title of the book?' Hugo asked.

'It's about houses,' she said, rummaging in her bag. 'It's got beautiful pictures. I thought maybe if I get the book I will get the house. Anyway, it's a beautiful book. Have you seen it?'

'What kind of house would you like?' I asked.

'Oh, not like the ones around here,' she said. 'A wooden house with polished floors and balconies and dormer windows. A house that wouldn't disturb the nature spirits too much.'

'The what?'

'You know . . . '

'I see.'

'The farmers here are driving them away. Bulldozing and rooting out the fields like anything. It's a shame.'

'The countryside is losing its character right enough,' said Hugo.

'Oh yes,' she agreed enthusiastically. 'This was the last place in Europe where they were safe. Where are you going?'

'The Kirwin's place. Derrylea House. Do you know it?'

'I go there now and then. Not to the big house of course, but to the woods and round the lake. It's like another world there.'

I wanted to ask her what she was living on, but she pointed to an old quarry and said her caravan was parked in there. There wasn't a house in sight for miles. All you could see were grey rocks, yellow furze and blue, distant hills.

'Aren't you lonely here?'

'Oh no, not when I can feel them around me. Safe journey now, and God bless!'

Again it seemed as if her farewell had come copied from somebody else. She said it deliberately and with pride, like a child imitating adults.

'I bet she's a witch,' said Hugo. 'Probably dances naked at full moon on top of turf stacks.'

We spent the rest of the journey to Lough Derrylea wondering what she ate for dinner. Nettles? Black-berries? Mushrooms? There wasn't a shop for miles and miles and the only thing she seemed to have brought from Galway was a book. Maybe she kept hens? But what would she feed them on? We racked our brains but couldn't come up with an answer. Perhaps she didn't exist?

It was pleasant to think that it wasn't our problem after all.

The rain got tired at last. We drove through a snare of amber and honey light. It beguiled us. It elided every-thing. Mallard quacked contentedly on Lough Derrylea and the tall Scots Pines round the house exuded self-confidence.

Jack and Tracey were sitting under the catalpha tree on the front lawn.

'Holy Sweet Jesus,' said Hugo. 'Will you look at that!'

They were both dressed immaculately in white and looked as if they had just stepped out of a Bergman film. Jack had lost his belly and the bags under his eyes. The crease on his linen slacks was sharp as a knife. Tracey had her blonde hair up and her blouse down. She looked ten years younger, wheat-brown and well caressed.

We were intruding. I could see that straight away.

'Where on earth have you been?' asked Hugo in mock anger. 'And why don't you answer the phone?'

Tracey waved her hand dismissively and tugged Jack's sleeve to draw him away.

'Isn't it lovely?' she said to nobody in particular. 'Isn't the light absolutely gorgeous?'

I could sense Hugo's shudder.

'Have you come for some strawberries?' asked Jack. 'Help yourselves!'

'You both look great,' I said to cover my embarrassment.

'We're having a lovely time, thank you.'

Jack put his arm round Tracey's waist and turned indifferent blue eyes on us.

'It's been very good to see you,' he said.

'Well, I'll be damned,' said Hugo furiously as they walked away.

'No, no, no. Nothing like that at all, old chap,' Jack smiled, turning his head.

We watched them, flabbergasted, as they ambled off in the direction of the lake. I have a distinct memory of the flounce of Tracey's long white dress sodden in the wet grass.

'I don't think they even recognised us,' I said to Hugo. 'They must be as high as kites.'

'Well, let's get at the strawberries at least,' said Hugo. 'That is, if the dogs let us.'

But there were no dogs to be seen anywhere. The strawberry beds were a mess. Nobody had bothered to pick them for weeks. The blackbirds and slugs were having a feast.

'I won't leave this place without a drink,' said Hugo testily.

We tried the hall and kitchen door but they were both locked. Even the conservatory was jammed shut. We understood why when we peered through the glass. It was bursting with sunflowers and cannabis plants.

'Tracey's harvest is doing nicely,' said Hugo sourly.

Suddenly I felt old and unloved. I thought of Tracey and Jack wandering around the lake in their white gear, idiotically happy and puffing the magic dragon. It was unfair. We were the ones that were supposed to be happy.

'Let's get out of here,' said Hugo.

I knew that he envied them too.

In the car we agreed that Tracey and Jack deserved a break. Anyway, it was probably the last fling before the final crash.

We drove in silence. I was almost relieved when Hugo stopped to pick up a shabby old man who was gesturing awkwardly by the side of the road. Before he got in he poked his head suspiciously through the window and examined us carefully.

'Are ye Jehovahs?' he asked aggressively.

'What Jehovahs?'

'OK so. If yer not Jehovahs you can take me as far as Moycullen.'

He settled himself vigorously in the back seat.

'Them Jehovahs have the country plagued. Have you seen them round yeer way at all?'

'No.'

'They should be lined up against the wall and shot, every last one of them. Man, woman and child. They have me persecuted. Saving your presence Mam, but I wipe me arse with their Bible.'

'Why do you do that?'

He bristled and waved his hand in my face.

'Because I'm a good Catholic, that's why. Them buggers have been trying to get me for months. Three times in the last fortnight they tried to run me down on the road. But I was too quick for them. Wanst I hurt me leg jumping into the ditch. Look at that!'

He rolled up his trousers and held up his leg.

'You should have that seen to.'

'Is it coddin' me y'are? Them nurses and doctors are all Jehovahs on the quiet. A man like me wouldn't be safe with them. What are ye doing anyway in this part of the world?'

He was suspicious again.

'We've been to Derrylea House.'

He shook his head. 'Did you ever hear the beat of it? And all the money they had! Wouldn't you think now that people like them would be content?'

'Who?' I asked. 'Are you speaking about the Kirwins?'

'Who else?'

'They seemed happy enough to me when I spoke with them half an hour ago. I never saw them looking better.'

There was dead silence in the back of the car.

When I looked round I saw a cunning grin on his dirty, stubbly face.

'And you spoke to them you tell me?'

'Of course.'

'And what did they have to say to you?'

'The usual. Why are you asking?'

'Because you're a bigger liar than I took you for. Let me outa here. I'll go no further with ye.'

'What's the matter?' asked Hugo slowing down.

The old man opened the door and swung himself out while the car was still moving. With a scream he fell on the grass verge. We rushed out to help him.

'Get away from me, ye pair of fuckin' Jehovahs. Don't touch me!'

'Look here, we're not Jehovah's Witnesses, good, bad or indifferent,' said Hugo, helping him to his feet.

'I know your tricks. You're liars like all of them! Talking to ghosts. Ghosts don't talk!'

'What ghosts?' asked Hugo.

'Get away from me!'

'Do you mean Mr and Mrs Kirwin?' I pressed him.

The old man muttered something in Irish and limped away.

That's how we learned that Jack and Tracey were well and truly dead, just as we had suspected. Their bodies had been found in the lake by a party of German fishermen on the seventh of July when we were on holidays. Requiem mass was celebrated by Father O'Meara and the remains were interred in Derrylea chuchyard. The Kirwins were greatly lamented by their niece Miss Ellen Kirwin of Balreask House, Old Balreask, County Meath. Etc., etc.

It would be too much to say that we were saddened by the obituary notice in *The Connacht Tribune*. Somehow the prospect of Jack and Tracey's death had always been a relief to us, both during their life and afterwards.

Fuair se bás b'fhéidir nach raibh sé beo riamh.

Easter Journey

(1) Waiting

The buses are brazen today. They trundle past without the slightest intention of stopping. Sly-boots, pretending not to see me. Buttery eyes, greasy arses, wobbly torsos. Heaving and spewing water all over the place. They hate me.

My *Evening Herald* peels apart in the rain. I've read everything down to today's temperatures in Prague, Rome, Stockholm, Strasbourg, Venice, Warsaw, Zurich.

Dublin is suffering from a mid-Atlantic blocking pattern that's expected to last over the Easter Holiday period.

John Cronin doesn't give a fuck. He's speeding home to Oranmore in his new Honda CRX Coupé, with Pavarotti booming from the speakers. His hands, tanned by the Lanzarote's sun, thump the rhythm on the steering-wheel.

More and more shrouds join the queue. They rustle. They rustle and mutter obscenities. Whiff of sour wet something. Damp vinyl? Armpit? Definitely armpit. The rain draws it out. With the right kind of smell camera you could photograph blobs of it seeping out of them. Plasma of some kind. Or stink-auras. Standing in stink-auras, like Father. Poor Father. Daddy. Pappa.

> O treasure him Lord in your garden of rest
> For he was my Dad and one of the best
> Forget you Dad I never will
> For in my heart I love you still.

Never a day sick etc. The family sunk in etc.

> You closed your eyes dear Dad without
>   goodbye
> But memories of you will never die.

The shrouds come to life. Bulky and broad-browed above the traffic, the number 8 bus bears down on us. Ten to one it doesn't stop.

> Green Bus: Halt for us,
> Green Bus: Be gracious to us.
> Green Bus: Wipe away our cares.

It doesn't. I win.

The shrouds slump over a huddle of big-eared shopping bags. Another thirty minutes at least. Lots of time for impure thoughts. I've always been able to contract time with impure thoughts. Fr. Dooley said: 'Boys, you will be tempted by impulses, especially in the bath. When this happens, imagine yourself doing it to Holy Mary or your mother. Surely you could never bring yourself to continue?'

I could. There goes another frigging bus.

Cronin doesn't give a fuck. At this precise point in time he is smelling Chanel No. 5 on the nape of his wife's neck and working his left hand under her pink angora jersey. With the free hand he waves to his mother who is kneading wholemeal dough on the pinewood kitchen table.

Mother. I spent the whole morning trying to contact her. The curtains were drawn, the doors locked front and back, no sign of life anywhere round the house. Even the key on the long blue string she keeps buried in the flower pot under the garden seat was missing. I tapped on the windows with a coin. 'Mother! Are you there? It's me!'

Perhaps she forgot to put in her hearing aid? Perhaps she was dead? I sat on my bag by the orchard door and waited to see. The Virginia creeper dropped red webbed hands on my head and shoulders. The orchard was a chaos of naked limbs half eaten by young green nettles. A lewd scrub of blackcurrants and gooseberries fumbled round the plums and pears. The apple tree where we had the swing was bent over like a Shila-na-gig holding open a moist black cleft for all to see. I took out a squashed Easter egg from my bag and put it on the window-sill.

'What do you think you're doing coming round the place like this?'

She stood in the doorway wrapped up in three pullovers, a black scarf knotted round her head, her long blue nose dripping. She had a black plastic bag over her shoulder.

'Why didn't you come on Holy Thursday like you said you would? I had the yard light on for half the night. Have you any idea of the expense? You think I have nothing better to do than to wait up for you? You're very much mistaken.'

She emptied the bag into the rubbish bin. I caught a

glimpse of old yellow photographs and my father's IRA medal mixed up with the dead cinders and cabbage leaves.

She started to drag the bin to the front gate.

'No, I don't need your help. Or your Easter egg either. People have to do for themselves. If it wasn't for the neighbours I'd be dead long ago. You're never around when you're wanted. That's the thanks we get for educating you. Where did we go wrong? There's nothing in the house. Be off with yourself. Ask that slut of yours to look after you. Hell isn't hot enough nor eternity long enough to punish the pair of you. It's a blessing you're not let next nor near your poor children. With a scut like you for a father God only knows how they'll turn out. But don't worry. Some day soon you'll know the damage you've done. And then it'll be too late. Be off now and close the gate after you.'

I was glad she spoke to me. I don't remember her speaking to Father very much. Instead of saying something she just looked at him. She gave him all sorts of looks. They stayed together because they prayed together. Now the chain is broken.

> We cannot bring the old days back
> When we were all together
> The family chain is broken now
> But memories live forever.

(2) Waiting

I'm sitting on the top deck restored to grace. One of the elect to be allowed to enter through the flaming door. In the land of waiting anything that moves rules. The shrouds are steaming quietly to themselves, their bottoms gratified. Stuck to the window beside me is 'The bus workers' reply to the management provocation:

> Go slow
> Go slow
> Go slow
> Go slow'

The bus lurches to a halt. The rat-faced conductor pokes his snout into the upper deck and shouts we're not going any further. There's a go slow on this route. This is the last stop for today. Everybody off!

The shrouds descend to the street. They are silent. They form a queue. I take my place in the gap of time. The big-eyed Georgian houses opposite upbraid me and by bag. They despise me. They know the type all too well. Maybe Hitler was right after all, maybe people like me should be –

The lights comes on in the living room. John Cronin is down on all fours with his two laughing boys astride his back. 'Gee up, Daddy!' they cry. 'Faster, faster!' He loves the smell of their little hands and the feel of their well-packed bottoms.

> Forgive me Lord if I still weep
> For sons I loved but could not keep.

Sadly remembered by their grieving father, etc. I shouldn't have gone to see them. But after all it's Easter and my sons should have an egg from their father. Back in Galway I used to hide their eggs under the rhubarb leaves and say they were dropped there by a big yellow rabbit. Not any more.

They were sunk in armchairs watching a soccer match on BBC. They didn't look at me. Their bodies had the slack, sullen pose they take on whenever I appear, all dangling legs and arms. I gave them their chocolate eggs. Adam took his haughtily as if I were paying him back a small overdue instalment on a large debt. He put it on the floor without a second glance. Andrew stealthily began to unwrap his box. He said thank you in a way which showed that he was making a big concession for just this once. His accent had changed from Galway to Dublin.

'How's school, boys?'

'Fine.'

'Anything strange?'

'No.'

'How's your cold, Andrew?'

'Fine.'

'Have you played soccer recently?'

'No.'

'What's the team like this year?'

'Fine.'

'Will you spend a week or so with me in the summer?'

'No.'

Kim came in rattling her bracelets and bursting through her black striped dress. She's still an exotic delicacy, tender and poisonous as a *fugu* fish. In Japan they eat *fugu* for the thrill of it. You never know if it's going to be your last meal.

'Boys,' she said, 'tell your father to his face what you tell me behind his back. Go on, tell him.'

Adam turned to me and said, coolly, 'I don't want to see you again. Don't come here any more.'

Andrew swallowed and looked at me in confusion. He

couldn't say it. They'll get him for that. But he found a way out.

'What about our pocket money? You owe us for months and months. Fifty pounds each at least. Come on, pay up!'

Adam looked at him with admiration. So I took out my wallet and gave them five pounds each.

'Is that all?'

'Yes. What do you say?'

Silence.

'Damn you, what do you say?'

'I would prefer it if you didn't swear in my house,' said Kim, the poison sack swelling in her goitre.

'OK. I'm going. Give me a hug, boys.'

'I'm watching the match, do you mind?' said Adam.

Andrew fended me off with his arm. 'It was fifty not five pounds. You cheated us again!'

(3) Waiting

The shrouds grow restless. One after another they detach themselves from the queue and drift into the dusk. I lift my bag and follow them. Those who remain stare into the haze with triumphant hopelessness. Five hundred years hence archaeologists will find their rain-washed bones orientated in the direction of Drumcondra.

Cronin doesn't give a fuck. He's lolling on a Laura Ashley sofa and flicking through The Irish Times. *'Sweet Jesus,' he says to his delectable wife who prances around in a black kimono, 'Sweet Jesus, there's another bloody bus strike in Dublin. The country is bolloxed, what?'*

I wonder if I will get to see my father before he goes to sleep. The nurses are strict about not waking him. Not that it makes much difference, awake or asleep. He is crumbling. He smells of leaf mould and wild garlic. He has forgotten everything except four questions which give him twenty-four ways of conducting a conversation.

'How's business in Galway these days, Malachi?'

'Fine,' I'll answer. 'A little down on last year but that's only to be expected.'

'How's Kim and the boys?'

'Fine. The usual colds and flus. It's all this rain. They send their love.'

'Do you think we should join the EEC?'

'We have been members of the EEC for the last umpteen years.'

'Is that so?' he will say and drift into puzzlement.

And I'll take out the last chocolate egg and put it on his bedside table and he will look at it intently for ages as he does every time I bring him something and then he will turn to me and say: 'Is it Christmas already?'

> Father dear you're with me here
> However far on earth I roam,
> It's nice to know we'll meet again,
> This world is not our home.

Níl sa bhás ach dul abhaile.

Genius Loci

Once upon a time there was a man and a woman. He was a difficult man. But a good man. She was a difficult woman. She loved to sleep on his broad chest. He loved the feel of her long skinny flanks against his right thigh.

Every morning when she got up she spat three times over her left shoulder (as was the custom in her part of the world) and only then began a new day. He, on the other hand, lay on in bed for an extra twenty minutes or so letting the weariness pool into his buttocks and then seep out of him into the mattress. His heart was like an empty nut and as he lay there he said to himself: 'I can't go on any more.' But he went on. His heart was like an empty nut and his soul was leaking out of him but he got up and plugged the holes in himself once he heard the woman rattling the dishes grudgingly in the kitchen sink.

He drove to his work on a claw and a curse. She stayed at home cooped up in the attic which looked out over Galway Bay and painted her cycle of watercolours. They were called *The Murderous Innocence of the Seas Nos X[1]*,

X^2, X^3, X^4, X^5, X^π. This is what they did, day in, day out, rain, hail or shine.

But one evening when the man returned from work he found the woman standing in front of the window and peering out at the seeded dock-heads in the garden rusting in the rain.

'Well, my Tequila Sunrise,' he said, 'what's bugging you?'

'You must do something,' she said. 'This is not a good place. It's definitely not a good place for me. The wind is in my ears all the time. We're too close to the sea. We have to move out from this place or I'll go mad.'

'But where would you like to move, my Piña Colada?'

'Some place where the wind is less windy and the rain less rainy.'

And she opened *The Galway Advertiser* at Accommodation To Let. There people rented places they wouldn't live in themselves for all the tea in China. The advertisements said:

Knocknacarra area. Self-contained chalet with shower and fridge. Suit 2 gents. Reasonable. Call after 6 p.m.

or

Semi in Dangan Heights. Dual heating. All mod cons. Sleeps 6 workers. Particulars tel. 091-94061.

Most of the advertisements didn't apply because the man and the woman were neither 2 gents, nor 6 workers, nor reasonable. They wanted a place for an unmarried couple.

There were nine places available for unmarried couples in Galway. They were either caravans, converted garages or chalets. After the man and the woman had viewed all nine of them they returned to their windy house and the murderous innocence of the sea and tried to go on.

'I need the right place,' repeated the woman at breakfast, dinner and tea. 'I found the right man, the right work and now I need the right place.'

After many, many weeks of searching the man found a luxury apartment in Lower Salthill with big windows and glass doors in the living room. They moved in and the woman settled down. Or so it seemed.

Not a week had passed when the man returned from work and found the woman standing in the French window and peering out at the schoolchildren fighting on the grass.

'O my Knickerbocker Glory,' he said and embraced her. But she pushed him away with tears in her eyes.

'This place!' she said. 'It's like an aquarium. Everybody can see what I'm doing. I can't concentrate. They're watching me.'

And she strode out on the lawn, grabbed one of the children by the scruff of the neck and beat him up. She came back pacified and said meekly: 'All I want is the right place.'

Now I really can't go on, thought the man.

But he went on. He gritted his false teeth and started looking for another place.

After many, many weeks he found a charming mews on private grounds just off Rockbarton Road. The mews had character. The woman was delighted.

'Didn't I tell you?' she said. 'If at first you don't succeed,' and so on.

Alas, the very next day she got up in the morning and instead of spitting over her shoulder as usual, she sniffed.

'There's a smell in the house,' she said. 'A smell of old people.'

The man thought that by this time next year he would surely be pushing up the nettles.

The woman spent the whole day scrubbing and scouring the smell away. But when the central heating came on in the evening the rooms filled again with grannies' bad breath and granddaddies' piss.

'How's she cutting, my Cuba Libra,' asked the man with feigned joviality when he returned from work.

'I'm sorry,' said she in a haughty voice that stopped him dead in his tracks, 'but you're going to bring me to a Bed and Breakfast. I won't stay another hour in this stink.'

Next morning, instead of going to work, the man went to Blackrock to consider whether to commit suicide or take up all-year-round-swimming. Before doing either he decided to ring his rich aunt who had a very expensive house on Taylor's Hill. She was a daily communicant so the house was for married couples only. But the man was in luck. The aunt had just come back from Lourdes, where she had been cured of arthritis. In return she wanted to please Our Lady by being good to those who hated Her. Therefore she was kind to our man.

Fine, she said to him. You can stay in my house for £600 a month with one month's payment in advance.

So they moved in on the same day.

'Well, my Bloody Mary,' said the man. 'Now that we're bankrupt we can't afford moving any more. For fuck's sake, you'd better be happy here.'

But the woman wasn't happy. She couldn't find anything. Every time they moved house she lost a sketch, a pair of brushes, several pairs of knickers, a towel, a spoon, a shoe or two. Furthermore, she found that the place was against her.

'This house rejects me,' she said. 'I can feel it in the floors.'

She couldn't sleep for seven nights in a row. So she called in a water diviner and he found that the house was built over a blind spring. Little wonder she couldn't sleep. Little wonder she was edgy. Little wonder her man became impotent.

She got worse and worse. She couldn't eat, she stopped painting and she didn't wash her hair. She would just pace around the rooms in her dressing gown and repeat: 'I need the right place. There must be a right place somewhere. I can't stay here.'

She stopped liking other people and then she stopped liking herself. That's why she got cancer and died.

After her death the man had his first full day of peace and quiet in seven years. But during the night the woman came to him in his dreams and said: 'How could you bury me in Rahoon Cemetery? It's a frightful place!'

When the man woke up the following morning he thought it was only a dream, laughed and went about his business. But the next night and the next and the next night after that the woman came and nagged him. She wanted to be taken out of Rahoon and moved to Mount Jerome Cemetery in Dublin.

The man couldn't take it any longer. One night he went to Rahoon with a van, a wheelbarrow and a crowbar.

Snow was falling. It lay thickly drifted on the crooked crosses and headstones, on the spears of the little gate, on the barren thorn. It was a bit unusual for the middle of June. The man dug the woman up with the crowbar and drove her to Mount Jerome where he left her outside the main gate with a note in disguised handwriting pinned to the coffin lid: *She always wanted to be in Dublin.*

But the next night she was back again.

'They threw me in a pauper's grave and put the coffin upside down,' she sobbed. 'This country is not for me. Take me home.'

The man had always felt guilty about taking her away from her own people, from the golden steppes where she was young and beautiful and brilliant. It was a crime to bring her to the rain and the wind of the west of Ireland. He must make reparation. So he cashed in his Irish Life Insurance Policy, bought a mahogany coffin with a metal casing, disinterred her with the help of two unemployed biochemists and booked her and himself on a flight to Zaporoze.

On the way, somewhere between Ostrava and Cieszyn, when the stewardess was passing round miniature bottles of Wodka Wyborowa, the man looked up and saw the ghost of the woman emerging from the pilot's cabin. She wagged a blackened finger at him.

'*Durak*! I told you never to fly Aeroflot. It's a lousy airline. We're going to crash in five minutes.'

So the man gulped down his vodka as fast as he could and they crashed just as she said they would.

After the crash the man was reunited with the woman in a cyclodrome of whirling souls.

MAN   Together again at last. Are you happy in yourself?

WOMAN   I'm delighted. It's a great place! We're neither here nor there. Round and round we go!

MAN   We are in Purgatory.

WOMAN   We've arrived so.

MAN   In a manner of speaking, yes.

WOMAN   Well, shall we stay?

MAN   Let's stay.

[*They move*].

Níl aon tón tinn mar do thon tinn féin.

Shambala Way

I never really paid much attention to the newsletters from Edmund Ignatius MacHugh. Every so often he sent me a bulletin with updates on 'The Coming Ice Age', 'The Greenhouse Effect', 'The Rise of Ecotheology', 'The Fall of Patriarchal Man', and such like. It was only when MacHugh and his followers were almost roasted alive and Dhorn House burned to the ground that I took down the orangebox where I keep all my unread mail. Why I hold on to the stuff, God only knows. When I sorted out the sheets into seven piles according to colour I realised that they made up the spectrum of the rainbow.

The red sheets ranted 'Brace Yourself Banba!', the orange 'A Sacred Isle Once Again!', the yellow 'Take the Shambala Way!', the green 'Do It Yourself Cloudbusting!', the blue 'Fall In, Gnostic Guerillas!', the indigo 'Turn to the Irish Folk Soul!' and the violet 'Rise up, Lazarus!' The last newsletter was untitled. It was a plea for money to help prevent Edmund Ignatius MacHugh going to jail.

The summer of that year dripped with rain and

rumours. There was an American millionairess who believed MacHugh was the most important man now living. She had donated half a million dollars, no, a million, maybe ever two, to him and his Shambala Seekers. There was a love affair, there was jealousy, there was revenge. There were gales and rainstorms the likes of which we had never known before.

The countryside round Finvara seethed with execrations. It was MacHugh who had caused the downpour, MacHugh and his mafia below in the Big House. The sons of bitches should have been thrown back into the fire. The rain never ceased for a day even though the lads from the hurling team wrecked MacHugh's cloudbusting machine and endless rosaries were offered up for fine weather. Sergeant Ruane, who had studied the Prophecies of St Malachy, said that the wind and the rain were a sign of the shifting of the earth's axis. Ireland would be the first country to go under after California. He sold his bicycle, donated his Garda overcoat minus the chevron and silver buttons to the St Vincent de Paul and hung himself from a beam in the Day Room.

The intellectuals who met on Sunday afternoons in Paddy Burke's for chowder, brown bread and tea had a feast of unanswered questions. How to get a million dollars? Was madness a *sine qua non*? How come MacHugh pulled it off and the rest of us didn't? Was it really possible to change the weather or was it a new pishorogue? Was it true that MacHugh was off in the Burren Hills on a vision quest? What was this vision quest thing anyway? More pap for the dispossessed! They shook their heads, read *The Observer* and went back home to help the children with their exercise. The whole affair, they said, was atavistic in the extreme.

I spent the summer tracking down what was left of the Shambala Seekers. After the fire, they had scattered to the four winds in flight from a posse of Gardaí and lawyers. It took me a long time to persuade them to give me their version of what had happened. We don't have anything to do with journalists, they said at first. Journalists only twist everything. Who would understand anyway?

But I convinced them. I told them what a good communist had once said to me: 'That which is not written down does not exist.' Would they prefer that Shambala sink into the sump of folklore and spite? They wouldn't. But they refused to have their names or any details of their whereabouts disclosed. They wanted to remain incognito until their master returned to cure Ireland of its madness.

Dr P: I was in charge of Project Purification. Every morning I collected samples of the first urine passed on awakening by the Shambala Seekers. I sealed the bottles tightly, dated them, and let them sit on a shelf in the pantry to settle and cool. After a few days the urine would show a heavy cloud of mucus. The longer I kept the urine the more the cloud of mucus revealed itself. When it got especially dark I reported the fact to Edmund Ignatius. He would ask me to bring a batch of the bottles to the Library before evening meditation. There we would discuss how long we as a community needed to fast to rid ourselves of toxins. Usually we came off the fast just as soon as the urine in the bottles stabilised at the colour of a new penny.

B: You want to know what was so great about MacHugh? Mac was a Prophecy Man, that's what. He knew that the world is bunched. Ireland is bunched, every last one of us is tee-totally fucked up. So what's new about that? Every dog in the street knows as much. Now – what do you do about it? Most of us sit around on our arses and do sweet feck all. Mac was different. He set out to change himself first and then the world. And he paid the price. No, he was no ordinary Joe Soap. He was a warrior of the spirit. I know what I'm talking about. I was with him on the Holy Mountain.

It was like this. Mac and myself were doing time in Crumlin Road Jail. Nothing criminal. Mac got six months for inciting Crown troops to desert. I was inside for beating up the con man who ran off with the wife. I was only three months married at the time.

From the start I could see that Mac was a cut above the others. No bad language or drugs. At the same time he didn't take any bullshit from anybody. We talked a lot. When the others were watching TV or playing poker Mac was stretched out on his bed reading all these books he got from the Mothers' Union. He was a man with a big mind. I told him about my wife, how she bitched me and all so that I didn't want to go home from work any more. He put his finger on the problem straight off. People, he said, are exactly like vegetables. Every gardener worth his salt knows that you can't plant spinach with parsnips or onions with broccoli. They don't get along. They cancel one another out. Full stop. No matter how good the seed or the soil or the situation or the weather. They just won't thrive beside one another. There's no use in a parsnip feeling guilty and crucifying himself because he can't make it with a spinach. They have to separate. It's a law of nature.

When he told me all this I felt a huge weight fall from my shoulders. It made sense of everything.

Mac had his own way of thinking and doing things. If he got an idea into his head you couldn't budge him. Just before our time was up he asked me if I could help him with a little experiment when we got out. By then he could ask me for anything. I'd go through hell and high water for the son of a gun. It was very important and was just between the two of us. He was going to do a vision quest, same as the Red Indians. He wanted to find out what he should be doing with the rest of his life. When an Indian brave wanted to know his task he went to a holy mountain with one of his mates. He stayed there for three days and three nights naked as the day he was born, fasting and crying for a vision. If he was lucky, a bird or animal of some kind came to him and told him his duty. Then the brave could always call on this bird or animal when he was in trouble. I'm not asking you to believe it. It's what Mac told me. He wanted to have a shot at it for himself and he wanted me to go with him.

Brother K: There's poison everywhere. In the earth, in the air, in the water, in lovers' kisses, in mother's milk, in the bottle of stout even. Don't ask me why I'm drinking. It's in the mind above all. Everything is poisoned. And dense. Things are getting denser and denser, all the light squeezed out. Neo-patriarchal man is unable to discover the Divine in anything. What he sees outside is only his own blighted soul made visible. Dark man: dark universe. That's what MacHugh repeated over and over again, God be good to him wherever he is. Now don't ask me why I'm drinking.

B: On the day we were released the first thing we did was to go to the Army and Navy Stores. We bought a tent, sleeping bags, a pair of binoculars and a flask. Then we drove straight from Belfast to County Mayo in my old VW van. We pitched the tent in a quiet spot at the foot of Croagh Patrick. Mac said my job was to patrol the area and let nobody, but nobody, disturb him for three days and three nights. Then, very slowly, he stripped himself naked and went off up to the top of the mountain without a backward glance.

So I settled down as best I could to watch out for farmers or pilgrims. It wasn't easy. What was I supposed to tell them? That there was a naked man up there doing a Red Indian vision quest and that he might die if they disturbed him? No way. And what was I to do for the three full days and nights? When the mist came down and the wind shook through the hazel scrub I thought maybe Mac and myself needed to have our heads examined. It was a weird thing to hear him at night howling out for a vision. I was often tempted to leave base camp and go to see what he was up to. But he made me swear that I wouldn't go next nor near him, no matter what happened.

On the fourth morning I climbed Croagh Patrick with a flask of hot Bovril. When I reached the top I saw the damnedest thing. There were a dozen badgers lying in a

circle on the rocks with Mac in the centre fast asleep.
Real badgers, big and fat as seals, with a white stripe
down the head. They ran off when they got wind of me. I
was still stuck to the ground when Mac opened his eyes.
He took a long time stretching himself and scratching his
chest.

'For Jasus sake, Mac,' I said, 'say something.'

He winked at me.

'I've made it. I know what to do.'

If I hadn't seen the badgers with my own fecking eyes
I'd have never believed him.

J: Our Iggy had what he called an ideal morning. We got
up at six o'clock on the dot. No lying on in bed because
Iggy said that it only drew down bad thoughts from the
astral plane. We drank a cup of boiling water to purify the
system and did our meditations wrapped up in blankets.
Then we did our breathing exercise. First we took a deep
breath saying the names of the virtues we wanted to have.
We held it for a count of sixteen. Then we breathed out
saying 'I expel from myself the three faults contrary to the
three virtues.' We always had porridge for breakfast. No
sugar or milk. Just porridge and brown bread while Iggy
checked out our dreams. We had to learn how to dream
all over again from scratch. It wasn't good enough to let
dreams happen. You had to be able to know that you were
dreaming when you were dreaming. That was the first
step. If you could direct what was happening in your
dreams you could direct what was happening in your life.
I never managed anything like that myself but Maggie
did it every other night. You could see why Iggy chose to
sleep with her.

Then we all went to work in the garden Iggy had staked out in the back pasture. We grew our own bio-dynamic food, especially spinach, radishes, scallions and carrots. We made sure to plant them at the right phase of the moon. Iggy said that this was the way it was done in ancient Ireland. But people had forgotten the old wisdom. We were going to bring it back.

In the middle of the day Iggy gave us a talk. My job was to take it down in shorthand and type it all up for the newsletter. He would stand in the kitchen with his back to the Aga cooker and deliver his message to mankind. He liked to speak with the music of Mise Eire playing on the tape recorder. It would be on full blast, the waves crashing and all and he would have to roar to make himself heard above it. It was just great. He was like a Druid standing there and belting the stuff out. The gist of the message was that we should stop being parasites and live more in tune with Mother Earth. The Earth was being ruined and we with it. Somebody had to start somewhere and we had made a start in County Mayo. We had an old mimeograph machine we got on the quiet from the Garda Barracks. When there was enough material to make up a newsletter we turned out 1,000 copies. Maggie posted them – 300 inside Ireland and 700 all over the world. Iggy's and my dole, Maggie's children's allowance, even the odd few quid from the Vincent de Paul went for buying stamps.

Dr P: I had long suspected that the next phase in biocultural evolution had just begun. This has been made possible through the production of humanoid forms with an increasing number of neural connections between the frontal lobes and the high cortex. These new humanoid forms are the children of the spirit. Evolution is no longer physical but metaphysical.

Personal transformation! Mind remoulding body! This was the clue, as I saw it, to Ignatius's Cosmic Therapy. I was flabbergasted. I watched as massive bio-energetic blockages and psychological hang-ups disappeared in all of us, one by one. Ignatius himself was the best example. Within the space of a year he lost his patriarchal identity so completely that his handwriting changed and he could no longer write his old signature. None of his seven sons by his previous marriage could believe that this man was their father.

Because of my rational education I was the slowest. But bit by bit I began to move through my own phase of personal transformation. I was surprised to find that a large bunch of varicose veins which had developed around my testicles when I was a teenager suddenly completely disappeared. This enabled me to experience for the first time the orgasmic ecstasy of the full-blooded genital embrace.

J: Our Iggy's mind was always on higher things. He might be cleaning out the cowshed and all the time he'd be explaining about Constantine Nicholas Roerich or Count Ferdinand Ossendowski. You'd love to hear him talk and watch the way the grape in his hand became a man's spine or a harpoon or a gear lever or whatever it was he wanted it to be. He read all the time and made notes. There were stacks of books everywhere. Sometimes he got really upset by what he read and then we knew to keep out of his way. He was like a demon out of hell. In the middle of the night you'd be woken up with cursing and swearing coming from the toilet. He'd storm out with the book that upset him and demand that each of us get out of bed and read the bits that got under his skin. If you didn't join him he'd turn on you and say you were as bad as the others. I often wondered how he could be so bothered about what the books said and not care a hoot for other things. No proper roof over his head, no money, no job, two small children and the P.P. Father Herbert, accusing him of spreading paganism. But he never paid any attention to all that. First the image, then the thing, he said. Follow the Law of Manifestation. And that's just what happened. We might want a few laths to build a cloche and he would just hold them in his mind over-night. Next thing a load of timber would fall off a lorry right outside out house, nails and all. He always got more than he wanted of everything – seed potatoes, horse manure, rolls of fibreglass, cabbage plants.

Dhorn House came to him just as easily. It was on 23 June. I was out feeding the hens when Iggy called us all into the kitchen. He had a bit of paper in his hand and he looked like the cat that got the cream. It was just like him to say nothing for five minutes and to keep us on tenterhooks. Finally he hit the table with his fist, gave us a wink and shouted 'There's hope for humanity yet. Life on the dole is over! We're rich! Father Herbert can take a flying fuck at the moon!' That was the first and only time I heard him speak with disrespect of the clergy.

You'd love to see him there and then, stomping round the kitchen and shouting like a Red Indian. And well he might. An American millionairess wanted to donate $225,000 to our commune. She'd just read our newsletters and had decided Iggy was the greatest thing since the sliced pan.

After this everything went like a dream. Iggy had a vision when he was shaving at the kitchen sink. He saw a map of Ireland with a light coming out of the south shore of Galway Bay. A tree grew up out of the spot and its branches covered the whole land of Ireland. All the birds of the air came to roost in it.

'That's it,' said Iggy. 'I'll know the place when I see it.'

So we set out the next day on the bus to Galway and from there to Ballyvaughan. Iggy sat up in the front seat like a greyhound. Half-way to Ballyvaughan didn't he shout at the driver to stop and we got off. There were eight of us including the children on the side of the road. We watched Iggy feel around for a bit with his stick.

'As the crow flies it's about two miles thataway,' he said, pointing in the direction of the sea. We followed him down a crooked road, putting our trust in his vision and taking turns with carrying the children. Sure enough, at 4 o'clock we saw it. There was Dhorn House with 'For Sale' hanging on the gate. Iggy got down on his knees and kissed the ground.

B: Mac said that Dhorn House was the new spiritual centre of Ireland. As it stood it was no good. It had to be transformed. So boy did he get down to it. I've never seen so many fecking plumbers, carpenters, electricians and stonemasons in one place. They were tripping over one another. New furniture arrived by the lorryload from Navan, carpets, PVC windows, seven toilets – you name it, we had it. Mac supervised everything. He was the old MacHugh. You couldn't change his mind or anything.

When I said that we could do without orthopaedic beds and walnut tables he only snorted. 'No more scrimping or scringing. I won't have any plywood or plastic or hardboard hereabouts. A house should declare a man's spirit.'

To make a long story short we ran out of money.

It was Maggie who hit on the idea of inviting the millionairess over from Montana. So Mac wrote to her and asked her to be the Great Mother of the Shambala Seekers. Which is what we called ourselves from that time on. Sure enough she arrived on our doorstep two weeks later with another $50,000.

She was more of a grandmother if you ask me. She was over seventy and crippled with arthritis. So we fitted up the old carriage house as a luxury flat with its own central heating and a phone for her.

But was the bitch from Montana satisfied? No sir, no way. As soon as she arrived there was nothing but trouble in the house. It was too cold, it was too damp, the windows won't close, there's a draft under the door, it rains all the time, the toilet won't flush properly, the bath is too small, do this, do that. I was run off my feet trying to please her. And poor Maggie, a lady if ever I saw one, wouldn't hear a word against her.

Brother B: The world today is like a madly boiling pot of porridge. Events, big and small, are bubbling up here and there at a furious rate. At any moment the whole thing could boil over. Instability is piled upon instability. In the eyes of many the whole planet has been plunged in an ocean of uncertainty, despair and darkness. How long, O Lord, how long?

Give us a break.

Dr P: You've heard of DOR, I presume? Deadly Orgone
Radiation. Stillness and blackness spread over the land-
scape giving it a leaden, petrified quality. Certain indi-
viduals are especially sensitive to DOR. Some become
inexplicably sad. Others can't breathe. They feel as if
they are slowly seizing up inside. Many kill themselves.
Ireland is riddled with DOR. There are countless
victims.

A dead atmosphere has few streams of life-force in it.
But a correct cloudbusting operation creates and intensi-
fies the life-force stream. That's how Dr Wilhelm Reich
got tall green grass to grow in the Arizona deserts. We
followed his methods.

On 25 January we built our first cloudbusting machine.
I was given charge of compiling the Log Book Protocol
Data. We placed twelve 10 foot long by 1½ inch dia-
meter metal tubes on a wooden frame and pointed them
at the western sky. The tubes were grounded in the well
behind the house. The whole contraption looked like a
katusha battery.

At 5 p.m., precisely, rows of puffy clouds appeared all
over the sky. On the 27th the sky became cloudless and
the atmosphere developed a crystal-clear clarity which
none of us had ever experienced before. It was like
champagne. It was wonderful to watch the clouds blossom or vanish at the behest of our cloudbuster.

Our greatest feat of cloud engineering, in which I
played my humble part, was the reversal of Hurricane
Hilda. We picked her up as she approached sea area
Cromity. Another four hours and she would have

smashed into the west coast. But we managed to turn her round and pushed her back to Finisterre where she broke up. The weathermen were completely baffled. Read the reports.

Edmund Ignatius decided to celebrate this feat by inviting the locals to join us in dance and song. This was a big mistake. We should never have done it.

Brother B: You know what they called us? The Moonies! We threw a party. They came to spy on us! And you know what they did? Sent in the Drug Squad to search Dhorn House for marijuana and magic mushrooms!

One day a girl came to work in the house to help Maggie with the cleaning. You know what happened? A teacher in the convent school organised a fast by her classmates to save the girl's immortal soul! They were fasting against us!

Day after day the dark forces increased in power. We tried to protect ourselves by bathing Dhorn House in a halo of white light. We drew streams of fresh energy from the more mature trees about the estate. But they must have been watching us. One morning we woke to find all the outlying beeches dismembered and mutilated. That's gratitude for you. That's all the thanks we got for improving the weather.

J: Our Iggy paid no attention to the gossip. He asked us to carry on as usual, even if every man's hand was against us. But then something really awful happened.

I was hanging out the washing in the back yard when I saw this big huge black car pull up. It was really old-fashioned, the kind you see in Laurel and Hardy films. Two fellows in black suits got out and stood there looking at me. One of them was tall and Swedish looking. The other was much shorter with black hair and a crew cut. They just stood and stared. It was horrible. I can't describe it, but it was as if they were only half there. Do you follow me? Then they turned away and began to walk in the other direction. I never saw man nor beast walk like that before. They jerked one foot after the other like robots or somebody kneecapped by the IRA.

I could have sworn that the whole thing lasted only a few seconds. But when I got back into the house it was dark and tea was over. I burst out crying. Iggy made me a cuppa and asked me to tell him what happened very slowly from the very beginning. When I finished he stood up pleased as punch with himself. He clapped his hands and said: 'I knew it! They're after us. We must be getting very close.'

He wasn't one bit put out.

The two men I had seen were MIBs, Men In Black. I mean men is not the right word at all. MIBs are only imitations. You can recognise one straight off by a sort of half-finished, old-fashioned look, a bit of the face sort of missing, an old car, a strange hat or funny movements. They have appeared to thousands of people the world over who have got close to Shambala. MIBs are up to no good. Iggy said they came from the lower elementals and they wanted to put a stop to us. He really surprised me that time, I can tell you. After all, we were in danger of our lives. But it looked to me like he was proud of the visit.

B: Every Sunday evening we got together in the library to meditate on the Celtic Folk Soul. Mac's idea was that

Ireland's time had come again and that we would soon be the light of Europe. To speed things up we needed to be in tune with our Folk Soul.

Everything went fine till the Great Mother started passing into her trances. She would shudder and shake and say that the Power was flowing through her. She said the Celtic Folk Soul was calling on Mac to lead the way. I never heard such bullshit in all my life.

She wanted to force Mac into being some sort of guru. But he would have none of it. He told her that a guru is a man with a psychopathic streak who wants to have power over others. But nothing would stop her. Many's the time I caught her winking gamely and making eyes at Mac and putting her scrawny old hand on his knee. She was like a seventeen-year-old with fire in her knickers. Mac tried to contact her Better Self with his Higher Self but it only encouraged her leers and whispers the more.

It went on like this for months on end. The Great Mother became a great pain in the arse. She picked on all of us but Maggie was her favourite victim. She often kept after the poor woman from first thing in the morning till last thing at night. When I mentioned it to Mac he wasn't a bit upset. He said that the struggle between the two women was a symbol of the larger battle going on on a planetary scale between the world of evil and the world of good. Like I said, Mac had his own way of seeing things.

After she got a raspberry from Mac, the Great Mother started slipping out to the pubs for a bit of consolation. The gobshites below in McLaughlin's were only too glad to hear the worst of us. She told them that Maggie was a Mayo whore and that the doctor was changing the climate of Ireland with his cloudbuster. Worst of all, she told them that it was me that was responsible for freeing badgers from snares round the place. That drove them fecking mad. They had this idea that all the badgers should be wiped out because they were spreading TB to the cows. What she didn't tell them, of course, was that the badger was our totem animal.

Brother S: Lies! Distortions! Threats! Legal mumbo jumbo! All these and more were showered on us after years of struggle for the Solar Age. Who would imagine that the Great Mother, so generous at first, so full of pioneering spirit, would finally turn against us? What appeared to be solid became fluid like quicksand. The siege of Dhorn House began. It was led by the bully-boys Meehan and Meehan, Solicitors, acting on behalf of the Great Mother. They demanded that we vacate the property immediately and give it back to her.

The property! What they couldn't grasp was the esoteric aspect of ownership. As the person in charge of the legal correspondence, I felt obliged to tell them that when Ignatius, Maggie and I took control of Dhorn House, we joyfully handed over the real ownership of the place to the Celtic Folk Soul. The technocratic dinosaurs simply couldn't grasp the point. They laughed at us. They said we were out of touch with reality.

My letters on behalf of the Shambala Seekers were my last service to Ignatius. It is to his everlasting credit that, even in those dark days, his mind remained focused on the Heights. You see, he never had a deed drawn up transferring Dhorn House to himself or anybody else, never checked if he was getting good title to the estate and never signed any contract with the workmen. He just didn't do it, full stop.

Now, wasn't it worthy of the Warrior of the Spirit? Doesn't that speak volumes for his faith in human nature? Edmund Ignatius MacHugh placed everything in the hands of the Celtic Folk Soul.

Christ, give me a break.

J: I don't know what to think. The whole thing was so awful. But then maybe it was necessary. Maybe it was some kind of test of our spirit. Everybody has to bear their cross, I suppose.

Brother S: All right. I'll go on. The day after the repossession order was issued we all met in the library. Ignatius was like a Martello tower. Solid. Unshakeable. Blunt. Item by item he reviewed the situation for us and proposed the one and only solution. We all agreed – with the exception, I may say, of the doctor – that Dhorn House must not fall into the hands of the enemy. How could we let the spiritual centre of our country be desecrated by thugs and philistines? How could we permit the navel of Ireland to become a guest house for German anglers and French wildfowlers?

There was but one way to translate Dhorn House from the gross physical to the subtle realms. Yes, my friend, we destroyed it in order to save it. In this we followed an authentic Celtic tradition. Dhorn House lives on in the realms of light where no greedy hands can reach it. *Slàinte*!

Dr P: Edmund Ignatius insisted that I leave my scientific

records to be burned in the flames along with everything else. With all due respect to the man, I think it was the wrong decision. Before it was smashed up, I had recalibrated the cloudbuster and improved its drawing power by a factor of 6 per cent plus. We had made significant progress in the area of fasting and compatible eating. So much so that I was on the point of submitting an application to the Rolex Award for Enterprise in Switzerland. One really can't help regretting the loss of so much data.

The fire itself was a botched affair and nearly caused the death of us all. Contrary to my advice, Edmund Ignatius used methylated spirits because of its alleged purity. Yes, you can't always trust the mystic. Next time round we must work out a better solution.

I went to Finvara to take a few snaps of the ruins. It was raining as per usual. From the top of Abbey Hill, Dhorn Point poked a blunt finger out into the Atlantic. The promontory was bare and penitential, battened down by a saltire of stone walls. At the knuckle joint, the classical portico with its broken columns and gapped balustrade seemed like a wreck from another civilisation cast up among the higgledy-piggledy bungalows and cottages. I pulled up to the whitewashed gate lodge. It was daubed with graffiti:

MOONIES GET OUT! MACHUGH = SATAN
FUCK THE MAYO WHORE!
LANDGRABBERS! SHAMBALLS!
FINVARA CUSACKS–6 SHAMBALA SEEKERS–0

One by one the crude letters had begun to streak and

blur, slogans of a petty insurrection that had flared and dissolved again in the rain. Even the final score was wrong.

Deacair goirriad a chur as an dstor ina bhfiuil sé.

How Slattery Tricked His Mother
Into Touching Him

This time it wasn't a woman that was the cause of Slattery's trouble. It was the fall of the People's Republics in Eastern Europe. Poland, Hungary, Czechoslovakia, Bulgaria, Rumania – one after another they deserted him. Such betrayal, such exposure! All the reactionary arseholes in Galway crowed over his embarrassment. They shook their fat heads in mock sympathy and quoted Havel at him.

Slattery passed off their gibes in dignified silence and in expensive Einhorn shirts which he wore as an act of defiance. All his life he had been loyal to the causes of socialism and transcendence. Both made him shockproof against anything that happened outside his own head.

In January 1990 he began to crack. He went through a series of rapid transformations. At first he bore himself like a Cabbalist, haughty and waspish in the conviction that he alone possessed the secret of the true socialism.

Then he was a wounded *commandante* in a beleaguered city. He staggered through desolate streets, barely able to stay on his feet as blow after blow rained down on him. Finally he was just a cranky old hen from the Legion of Mary. He repeated old phrases, rummaged for old icons, squeaked his big 'No' through pursed lips, forever virtuous.

With the fall of the Sandinistas in Nicaragua he collapsed entirely and went to visit his mother in Kells. She was the only one that loved him.

One last fit of fervour struck him on the bus home. He threw back his shoulders, raised his chin and displayed a dauntless profile to his fellow passengers. He was a Hero of the Retreat. All over the world, on buses, trains and bicycles, on camel-back, horse-back and mule-back, there were comrades like him who had lost a battle but not the war. But then the Abyss opened and the air went out of him. It was neither the Abyss of Pascal nor the Abyss of Dostoevsky. It was neither bottomless nor infinite nor majestic. Rather, it was bothersome, like anal itch, and too shallow to fling oneself into. It was Slattery's Abyss.

He almost cried when he found that his mother wasn't at home. He was desperate to talk to her, to feel her fussing around him, to have her make him a cup of cocoa, put a hot water bottle into the spare bed and say, accusingly as always, 'You haven't said the rosary.' Tonight he promised himself he would say a decade of the Sorrowful Mysteries.

He couldn't bear being alone. He had to find her immediately. She never visited the neighbours so she could only be in town doing the messages. Off to town then.

He walked briskly from shop to shop in search of her. Wary that anybody would stop him and ask questions he adopted an air of I'm-in-a-hurry-so-don't-delay-me. Then he saw her through the window of the Royal Meath Cafe, sitting alone at a table and eating a cake. As simple as that. Why then did he feel such terror?

She could be any old woman with nobody to talk to, spending the leftovers of her pension on a little treat for herself. She had raised five children, she was eating her mangey doughnut at a dead, tubular steel table, and she would soon die. And then there would be nothing left for him to connect to when all the lines were down. It was the first time he had seen her like that: alone, anonymous, redundant. He shivered. Through the glass he could feel the air around her frozen solid.

When he stood in front of her, she was at first puzzled and then, he thought, ashamed. He wasn't sure if she was ashamed of being caught unawares or if she was ashamed of being seen with him. Nobody in *her* family, she used to say, ever needed psychiatric help. Or mixed with communists for that matter.

'Seamus, is that you? Have you come all the way from Galway?'

'Right place, wrong son. It's Bernard.'

'To be sure. Here, have a cup of tea. You must be tired out of your wits. All that journey!'

She still had a 1920s sense of the distance between Galway and Kells.

She waved to the waitress but the girl deliberately turned her back.

'That slut wouldn't sell sovereigns. She's such a sour puss.'

'Its OK, Mother. I'll have something later.'

He was confused. His mother was completely oblivious to the pain she should have felt at being slighted like that. It seemed he had to suffer it for her.

He wished that they were at home and that he could hug her. Up till now he had always lived in a luminous place in his head which fed all his cravings. Now that the light had gone out he felt an abysmal need to touch and to be touched. But she sat there rambling on about Seamus, the two little girls and the sheepdog and how she couldn't stand that dog. Slattery unscrewed his ears and waited till her litany of venom petered out. The crisis in Rumania meant as much to her as last year's snow. No doubt she would regard his own crisis as a just punishment for his sins.

He walked her home, carrying her bags and trying to comply with her unspoken command that he make himself as invisible as possible. Occasionally she grabbed at him for support, fastening on the sleeve of his coat. 'Here Mother,' he said, again and again, 'take my arm.' But she pretended not to hear.

The house had the old familiar warm smell of decaying vegetation. Slattery filled his lungs with it and felt home at last. He couldn't wait, he simply had to hug her. He followed her like a dog from the stove to the sink and back again, chatting idiotically of this and that. His whole being, deprived now of the warm fraternity of struggling humanity and a sense of purpose, demanded this hug. Oh, how simple and natural it had been to embrace the comrades in Managua, Bratislava, Addis Abbaba. How many embraces, kisses, mutual toasts, impassioned speeches joined him to the proletariat of three continents! The revolution was sensuous, it was real. It was 1988 with Commandante Philippe in Las Palomas Nightclub, Havana! And now?

She avoided him as if she knew instinctively what he was after. Finally she stood in front of the gas cooker frying his favourite Lorenzen's sausages.

'It's great to be home, Mother,' he said, putting his arm around her shoulders. She stiffened on the spot like a patient on a dentist's chair.

'Set the table,' she said and moved quickly to the sink.

Slattery howled inside and set the table for four. Blindly he followed the old routine: a plate for himself, a plate for the wife, two plates for the boys. His mother looked at him accusingly.

'What do you think you're doing? Have you gone soft in the head on top of everything else?'

The years of revolutionary struggle stood to him. He was determined to get this hug. He kept watching her, waiting for a weak moment. Over tea he tried to soften her calcified soul by subterfuge. He talked about Daddy, about her skill with plants, about himself when he won the scholarship to St Finian's. Once or twice she seemed ductile, but a premature move earned him an elbow in the ribs.

A horrible realisation slowly dawned on Slattery. His own mother was untouchable. Worse, she had never touched *him*. It struck him now that he could not ever recall being kissed or hugged by her, not even patted on the shoulder with a good boy yourself! All her feelings were invested in plants. She was gentle with sweet williams, lupins, dahlias, daffodils and tea roses. Her devotion to thyme, lemon balm and rosemary was almost maternal.

'Look,' she would say softly, 'look at this little one!' and point to some nameless bit of greenery trying to push its way up through the John Innes mixture. Her eyes would fill with an affection she could never muster for an animal or human being. Only the drab sparrows she fed on the kitchen window-sill inspired the same tenderness. At last he knew why. She could minister to them without touching.

Now that he saw her frigidity in all its glacial bleakness he was determined to save her. He would humanise his mother! He would beguile her into touching him! That much he would do for her before she died.

He watched her carefully. Her routine was very simple. She got up at six o'clock in the morning, checked the weather and the sky, made herself a cup of tea and went back to bed. Now that there was a man in the house she felt safe and slept until ten. When she rose again she complained that the day was half gone and set to work in the garden. He could never see any traces of her labour except a small pile of weeds or a few twigs. But she always returned to the kitchen fresh and full of affectionate reproaches.

'You read to much, Bernard. Throw away them books and newspapers. Get out into the fresh air. Take deep breaths.'

And she would demonstrate, inhaling and exhaling, at the open door.

Occasionally he felt guilty about spending his days

listening to the news and reading newspapers. But when he offered to do something round the house, even so simple a thing as washing the dishes, she would protest.

'You have other things to do, Bernard. Sit down there and go on with your reading.'

But the pages were pure torment. Slattery couldn't tolerate a sentence with more than five words. Complex and compound structures were the façades of megalomania. Long paragraphs were Potemkin villages. His faith could stretch to subject, verb and object, no more.

In the afternoon she watched the children's TV programmes. She sat in front of the set with greedy attention, chortling and smiling happily to herself. She was so used to being on her own that she forgot all about Slattery's presence in the room. The screen was blurred and hazy but she made no effort to sharpen the focus. When Slattery tried to correct the picture she got angry and told him to leave her things alone. Watching TV with a blurred screen was a bribe to whatever mad God she believed in. It was the price she paid for indulging herself.

After tea she said the rosary, offering it up for her dead parents and old neighbours, her children, wherever they were, and her grandchildren, the Pope's Intentions, for all that we have and all that we are, to help Bernard find peace of mind and Daddy find eternal peace. Then she read *The Irish Independent*, usually three or four days out of date, and invariably fell asleep over it. She would wake with a start, make herself a mug of hot milk and ginger, and go to bed. Her last words were always the same: 'Say your prayers, Bernard, and we'll hang that door tomorrow.'

As the days passed she grew more and more remote from him. She got used to having him round the house. The indifference that followed her initial excitement at his homecoming made the hug even less likely. In the evenings Slattery slumped in the armchair where his father had slumped before him. He sat there mute and full of grief until he too fell asleep.

One such evening they were watching 'The Late Late Show'. As usual she was cutting the women guests to ribbons: 'Will you look at the gimp and get-up of that one.' Or: 'I'd put manners on that scut if I had my hands on her.' Then, all of a sudden, she grew quiet and intent. A woman healer was being interviewed. The camera showed a close-up of her hands. She had four well-defined bosses where the fingers joined the palm. These, she said, were the marks of the true healer.

Slattery saw his mother looking furtively at her own palm.

'I think I have it too,' she announced.

'Show me,' he demanded.

She bent back her palms and held them up to the light.

'Look at that! I always knew I had a gift!'

She said it in a way that suggested she had been fighting the gift all her life. And yet, at the same time, she seemed deeply moved by her discovery, as if her life made sense after all.

Now, at last, at the eleventh hour, his chance had come.

'Fantastic! Why don't we try it?'

She glanced at him apprehensively.

'No.'

'Look. It's dead simple. I've got an awful headache.
Who knows, maybe you can cure it? Let's have a shot
at it!'

'Don't be silly! Do you have any mending?'

'Come on! Let's try it.'

'I hope the Lord gives me mending at the Gates. I like
mending.'

His father's voice rang in his ears: *Bitch out of Hell.*

'Stop that rubbish about mending. Remember how
good you were with Daddy when he was sick?'

She hesitated. It was true.

'And with me when I had the meningitis. Most kids
suffer with brain damage after it. And me? I'm as sane as
– ' Slattery looked for a comparison that would appeal to
her – 'as a parish priest.'

She began to withdraw again.

'It's not right to meddle with these things.'

'Look. I don't want you to restore my missing teeth or
anything like that. I have a headache. You can cure with
your hands. It's as simple as that.'

'Go away.'

But she was weakening. Throw the Gospel at her now.

'Remember the man in the Gospel who buried his
talent in the ground?'

She looked at her hands again. God but she was slow.

'All right. Just this once.'

Slattery set himself low in the couch. For a moment
she stood in confusion, as if wondering how to start.
Then she picked up her shawl and drew it around her
shoulders like a stole. Hieratically, she approached her
son with her arms outstretched and held her hands an

inch above his head. He could hear her muttering prayers to the Virgin Mary on his behalf. Will she or won't she?

Her bony old hand rested on his head impersonally, with a professional assurance. He felt a glow of heat on the top of his skull. He tightened up inside. His heart was thumping in his chest and his throat went dry. He was a boy again, kneeling in front of the priest, about to receive Holy Communion.

'Did it work?' she asked matter of factly, stepping aside.

'A bit.'

Slattery's voice quavered as if he were about to burst into tears.

'Only a bit. You didn't hold it long enough.'

Next day Slattery stayed on in bed. At two o'clock his mother brought him beef tea and toast and an express letter. She was happy to have somebody to look after again and spoke to him tenderly.

'Keep yourself well wrapped up, Bernard,' she said. 'And call me if you need anything.'

Slattery opened the letter. It was a leaflet from the Communist Party of Ireland inviting him to a public meeting. It read: *In the light of the collapse of the Revisionist Traitor Regimes throughout Eastern Europe we hail the success of genuine communism in Albania! Communist Party of Ireland (Marxist – Leninist). Join us Monday 15 January, 8 p.m., beside the Cathedral.*

Slattery folded the letter pedantically and stuffed it in the pocket of his pyjamas.

'The lectures are starting,' he said. 'I have to be back.'

She nodded.

He decided to take the night bus to Galway. He couldn't bear to look out on the cold, psychotic fields of Meath, Offaly and Roscommon.

Is fearr beagán den mháthair na mórán den chléir.

The English Disease

For a description of location and general atmosphere you might like to look up Max Beerbohm's *Zuleika Dobson* or Jan Morris' *The Oxford Book of Oxford*. They're both out in paperback as far as I remember.

Everything that happened to Finnula confirmed my theory of *Puerophobia Brittanica*, the English disease. One of its symptoms is a fear of children. The other is a craving for the Dragon. As far as I can see, from the very first Saxon invasion, Englishmen have been given to tormenting children and slaying dragons. There must have been a bit of both in Finnula.

She took me by surprise. I read somewhere – maybe in Gustaw Alfons Bluszcz's *Celtowie: tragedia ginacego gatunku* – that Irish girls still went round on bicycles with one hand holding down their skirts and the other clutching their rosary beads. Finnula arrived at the College in a white Mercedes driven by a chauffeur who looked like Joseph Stalin at Yalta. I was checking my mail in the Lodge – bad news as usual – when I saw a skinny melusine swaying in the Front Quad. She was swaying and making bewildered grimaces while Stalin piled expensive trunks and leather suitcases beside her. She wore tomato-red pleated shorts over black tights, a black V-neck blouse showing a frilly black bra and a floppy red hat.

'You wouldn't by any chance know where staircase three is, now would you?'

The porter and I stared at her like cows at a painted gate. It took us a few seconds to answer her question.

Her voice was high and infested with elegant, half-swallowed diphthongs. The sound of those diphthongs filled me with respect and revulsion. At last a real Brit! I always wanted to improve my English by speaking to the English. But they wouldn't talk to me precisely because of my bad English. The only ones who talked to me were either American or Japanese or Welsh.

Apart from sharing the same staircase, Finnula and I had three things in common. We were bad Catholics, we hated to go back to our countries and we couldn't hold on to a man.

These things were of no use to me. I had counted on having an independent Protestant next door, somebody as self-righteous as mint tea and as uncomplicated as a table leg. Somebody who would lend me cigarettes, help correct my thesis and make phone calls for me in Queen's English. Instead there was this parasitic Catholic who was in the wrong country, the wrong clothes and maybe even the wrong body.

'I'm a virgin,' she hissed at me with hysterical self-reproach in the bar on the same evening. 'I've been a virgin since 1988.'

She was dressed in crocodile boots, tight jeans and a
pink bat-winged blouse which fell off her left shoulder.
She smoked ferociously without ever inhaling and furtively inspected male crotches. She divided men into those
who carried their penis on the left or on the right. The
left-thigh men were the nice ones. It must be some sort
of ancient Irish superstition.

I decided not to walk into the bogland of Finnula and
lose my shoes in her. But it was impossible. She had
invisible antennae which monitored my movements. I
was hardly in the door when I would hear the clatter of
her high heels on the stairs and her little voice calling out
'Wisla, are you there?'

Flaming in a silk salmon-pink night gown she would
burst into my room and fling herself on my bed. Then,
with a pillow clasped to her serpent breasts she would
talk about:

Her Moral Tutor
Her new Armani lipstick
Her irregular cycle
Her Moral Tutor
The advantage of contact lenses
The sexism of the English
Her Jungian dreams
Her oppressed childhood
Her Moral Tutor
Who was she?
Where was she going?
How to get there?
Was it worth going there anyway?
Who would know?

Did I know?

And such like.

She endlessly examined her reactions to things, testing her fears, petting her satisfactions, indexing her ennuis and anxieties, comparing the colours of her despairs, feeling the texture of her awakenings and probing the subtleties of her subtleties until she was pleased and perplexed with her own complexity. And I felt, not for the first time, that the sisterhood of women is a preposterous idea.

She loved me to oppose her. She was delighted when I said 'Finnula, my dear, you are utterly perfidious.' She pouted her lips and rolled her eyes and *was* perfidious. She gave me the mug of a mentor and advisor. I detested this role but found myself accepting it. In the same way I accepted my guilt when I was locked up during martial law. I was innocent, but it was enough that ZOMO treated me as a dissident and I became one.

There was only one thing I envied Finnula. Her family. I'm just a normal Polish Jew with the upper branches torched off the family tree. Finnula had real ancestors. They had been rotting away in the west of Ireland for seven hundred years. They were decayed and decadent, like a proper *szlachta*. There, near the bottom, were the syphilitic Plantagenets, over there, for balance, St Ferdinand, King of Spain. Near the top there was Finnula's grandmother. She had style. She gambled away the family castle – the lead from the roof, the great wooden staircase, fireplaces, chandeliers and all the trees of the estate. When she killed herself by eating a strychnine and cheese sandwich the wolves howled all night in

the Burren mountains. Afterwards the family moved to
the steward's house and stables. For years they had to
pee behind the bushes and eat spare ribs and black
pudding. But then a rich uncle died in South Africa and
they were back to the candelabras and ponies. There
were pictures of ponies with red rosettes on their bridles
over Finnula's bed.

Finnula's father was a Protestant atheist, her mother a
Catholic bigot. The mother's genes won out. All the
children had mental breakdowns, all of them victims of
victims. Finnula had her breakdown at some Catholic
boarding school for rich girls in Connemara. The big
girls stuck hairpins and swans' feathers up her orifices
and threatened to throw her in the lake if she told on
them. They called her Fishy Pussy and held their noses
when she passed.

She spat out her childhood all over the Persian carpet in
her room. I don't know why, but I felt no compunction
about stealing perfume and nail varnish from her dress-
ing-table. The last time such things were available in
Krakow was under the Habsburgs.

The fall of the Soviet Empire meant that I had less and
less time for Finnula. I spent sixteen hours a day at my
typewriter trying to improve a chapter on my theory of
the Patrimonial Pendulum in Soviet society. My thesis
advisor had just returned the chapter to me for the third
time with the same comment on every page: 'How do you
know this?'

As far as I could make out, Finnula spent most of the
day in bed. Like all women who are unhappily but
hopefully in love she was pouting in her boudoir. Some-

times, late at night, I caught her standing in front of a large mirror down the hall. She was pulling on endless blouses, skirts, dresses, shoes and underwear and shedding them just as quickly. She bristled with vexation. I had the same problem with my writing as she had with her clothes – taking up a sentence, changing it around, adding a clause, taking out a comma, throwing the whole lot away and starting all over again. Except that my stuff was cheaper.

Once she broke into my room for the loan of my feather earrings. She was wearing a shimmering ermine coat and when she sat down I saw that she was naked underneath. She was hungry for talk.

'I don't want to hear about anything,' I said. 'I'm working on the disintegration of the Soviet Empire and you are an adult woman. You know what you're doing.'

'I'm really very unhappy,' she moaned.

'I can't take the responsibility. Go and see a priest.'

She kicked over my waste-paper basket and left like an angry child.

She returned an hour later in tears and still naked under her fur coat. She collapsed on the floor, so full of misery and grief that I felt sorry for her. I made her a cup of tea, gave her a cigarette and sat beside her. She was immediately consoled.

'Wisla, what's wrong with me? Should I see a doctor or something? I'm all right as a woman, amn't I?'

And she opened her fur coat. Her thigh bones were sharp as set squares.

'Why are you going around naked?'

'He ordered me to. My Moral Tutor. I think he doesn't love me.'

It was no use my telling her she was stupid because she knew that already.

'Tell me about the Moral Tutor.'

Her green eyes lit up. She catapulted everything at me in three passionate sobs.

Well, the poor dear had fallen ill, something to do with the prostrate and she sent him a get-well-soon card which made him invite her for tea and she found to her surprise and much to her pleasure that her card was pinned to his mantelpiece and that he was most grateful and he talked about the hell of being an intellectual in Oxford. 'I am an island,' he said, 'within an island within an island,'and he showed her his collection of masks and boomerangs and they were all from New Guinea and he told her he was a Jew, which gave her gooseflesh all over because she had this incredible weakness for the Jews who are a brilliant intellectual race, aren't they? so when he touched her shoulder she thought of a baby, not making love or anything but having a baby and wasn't that superbly irrational of her?

She knew he had tremendous power over her and all he had to do was lift the phone and tell her to come over and she would come no matter what and she always did exactly what he told her to do, can you believe it, he would ask her to put something on, knee-length white socks or a tennis skirt or fish-net stockings and she would, she would, even though it was so much beneath her.

Sometimes he would lecture her on Lévi-Strauss in front of the Radcliffe Infirmary beside the statue of Neptune having oral sex with the oyster, sometimes he would take down her knickers and give her a spanking because it was good for her, sometimes he would give her a bath, paying special attention to her toes and bum but never but never did he kiss her, like that evening he wanted nothing to be between him and her which meant that she was to come naked to his room but when she arrived he looked at her sadly and told her to go home.

Now what in the name of all that's high and holy was wrong with her?

'It's clear as crystal,' I said. 'You are a perfect English couple. You were both perverted by your boarding schools. It's a textbook case.'

'But I'm Irish,' said Finnula.

'I can't see any difference.'

She was offended.

'For such a wise woman you can be very imperceptive. Of course there's a difference! No Irishman would ever get me to do what I did for my Moral Tutor.'

As far as I was concerned Finnula had put herself in a very unrewarding position. She had the reputation of being a whore but none of the pleasures. She didn't seem to care that half the College was gloating over her supposed debauchery. Worse, she was totally oblivious to the effect that her long hair, short leather skirts, low neck lines and crocodile shoes had on men.

The effect was such that the dons invited her for dinner in the Senior Common Room at the end of term. She should have known not to go. The last person to receive that kind of invitation was a black professor of feminist studies from Tanzania.

Several lurid versions of this dinner circulated in the College. One maintained that it ended with Finnula dancing an Irish Jig on the table and the Fellows looking up her skirt. A second had them all playing doctors and patient until dawn. Still another described a game of strip poker over the port.

'Bastards and bitches!' said Finnula. 'Nasty, vulgar lies! The truth is so much worse.'

And she told me the truth.

When she entered the SCR she noticed that she was the only woman present. There were five of them against her in her green mottled dress and red stockings.

'Sit down,' said the Senior Tutor, 'and try not to fidget.' He took her handbag with all her treasure in it and put it on the floor beside him. The others sat around in their gowns and evening suits looking at her drunkenly over the silver. She felt threatened by their clean-shaven red faces, piggy blue eyes and the sickly odour of tobacco, eau-de-Cologne and venom. The venom was dormant but somewhere in the room she could feel it becoming tumescent.

The Moral Tutor whispered in the Bursar's ear and looked at Finnula as if he were describing her anatomy. The Bursar whispered to the Dean, the Dean whispered to the Chaplain and the Chaplain said grace.

Soup was served by a dwarf with big red whiskers and no eyebrows. He barely reached to the top of the table. Nobody spoke. They just slurped and slurped away at their soup. Now and then one of the dons would stop, wipe his lips slowly and look at her with a question in his eyes as much as to say: Where did you come out of? The Bursar had a filthy habit of sticking his tongue out and licking his upper lip.

After the soup the Senior Tutor said: 'Now Finnula,

we are here to assess your standard of excellence, a quality in which I may say you're extraordinarily lacking. If we are severe with you, we mean it. If we are condescending, we mean it. Do not be under any illusion.'

He gestured towards the Modern History Tutor who held out her term paper and dropped it page by page on the table in front of him.

'This – shall we call it prose? – has a hormonally determined character. I can find in it little by way of logic, argumentation or coherence. The comparison between De Valera and the Shah of Iran does little justice to the Iranian.'

The dons he-hawed discreetly. The slayer in them was roused.

The dwarf came in with a huge silver tray of baked pigeons and chips. The table fell silent while he served the food. He did it awkwardly because of his height and the dons made no effort to make his task any easier. Finnula felt a sudden tide of sympathy for him; she said thank you several times in a sweet voice.

The pigeons were even more harrowing than the soup. Again, nobody spoke and all she could hear was gnashing and sucking and crunching. Suddenly it occurred to her that the dons, silence had a deeper meaning. And their voracity, it too had a meaning. They were telling her something. What could it be? But of course! The dons were devouring her! She felt her breasts and shoulders disappear down their gullets. They carved her expertly, carefully separating the bone from the flesh and chewing every last fibre with intense concentration. There was less and less of her.

'And now for dessert,' said the Senior Tutor rubbing

his hands. The dwarf wheeled in a tray with Grievous Angel and chocolate mousse. Finnula waved it away. She felt nauseous.

'Finnula, eat your dessert,' barked her Moral Tutor.

'Yes,' added the Bursar. 'We do insist that you eat your dessert like a good girl.'

All five of them put down their spoons until she started. She didn't have the strength to oppose them. Just as she was about to put a spoonful in her mouth she felt a hand slide along her thigh. Her horror subsided. Oh, God, she thought, at least somebody thinks I'm attractive. She looked around to see who it was but all hands were on deck. Then a second hand tried to pry apart her knees. As she leaned sideways to see who was molesting her, the table erupted with questions.

'Finnula,' probed the Dean. 'Isn't that a Scottish name? Macpherson and all that?'

'You've read Said on Celticism and Orientalism, I presume?' asked the Chaplain.

'Hardly,' said the Modern History Tutor. 'She thinks the Iranians are Arabs, don't you, little Finnula?'

'I never,' said the Bursar. 'Now my dear child, the fact that the Irish are Catholic doesn't mean they're Italians, does it? You've certainly heard the comment of the Duke of Wellington?'

'Indeed!' cried the Dean. 'Could you tell us, Finnula, who, in fact, was the Duke of Wellington?'

The face of the dwarf stared up at her from under the table. He looked like a sheik with the tablecloth draped around his head. He winked at her and made an obscene gesture with his index finger. Just then her Moral Tutor looked around the table and said: 'Gentlemen, does anybody have anything good to say about our lady guest?'

There was silence broken only by the Dean who released a short energetic burp. Finnula felt immensely grateful to her Moral Tutor for his question.

'By the by, have you found what you were looking for under the table?' asked the Chaplain with a knowing lift of his eyebrows.

The dons collapsed in sniggers. Finnula stood up and pulled down her skirt. Excited by her confusion the slayers looked up and regrouped. Then they swooped on her, their swords drawn and lances erect. And Finnula ran out of the room forgetting her handbag.

That was the end of the dinner.

I enjoyed Finnula's story and she enjoyed it too.

'I'm going to write a novel about it, it was so awful,' she said complacently.

I thought it was a very peculiar form of Irish revenge.

Finnula's passion for men who would defile her grew at every new encounter. She had no need to search them out. They came to her like passing dogs to a lamppost.

Roman Radziwill was one of them. Radziwill was the only person in the College with whom I could talk about the Eastern Bloc. He always had one hand on the pulse of Europe and the other on a girl's bottom. He was ruthless with both. His father was a count and his mother a baroness and his grandfathers had been hetmans in Lithuania. All of which, together with his hereditary ugliness and arrogance, made him more English than the English themselves.

Late in May Roman took to dropping in on me with a bottle of Crimean wine and we jeered at the science fiction of *glasnost*. Our raised voices lured Finnula down from upstairs.

'Why are you screaming at one another so much?'

'We are not screaming. We are having a discussion.'

'You Slavs scream at one another all the time. But I like it. It's so spontaneous.'

Roman was as predictable as John Paul II getting off a plane in a new country. He stood up, kissed Finnula's hand and begged her forgiveness in a Queen's English that squelched with sperm. She went limp as she listened to him.

I was too old for all that.

A few days later Finnula came to me with what she called a delicate problem.

'Roman wants to sleep with me,' she said.

'I can't see any problem.'

'But he's such an impossible reactionary. You're bad enough with your theories, but he's so much worse!'

'You're not going to sleep with his theories, I presume.'

'Well, I suppose not. Besides, I think I can forgive him because he's from a communist country. But the real problem is something else. You see, I told him the truth. I mean I told him I'm a virgin.'

'That, my dear, was a mistake. He must have been awfully distressed.'

'He was disgusted. He said it was out of the question. He couldn't carry the burden. I would have to find somebody who would initiate me into that sort of thing and then come back to him. We spent hours and hours together last night wondering who might do it. Do you know anybody?'

I didn't. I imagined how stupefied Roman must have been. Led on by rumours he had doubtless been greasing his gun for an easy Kama Sutra with the Serpent of the Shannon. For a man of his experience in debauchery to make such a mistake was a terrible *faux pas*.

'What about the Captain of Boats?' I said in order to say something. 'You know, the American with the beard. He looks at you with lust all the time.'

'Oh Wisla, do be serious. It has to be an intellectual. And a European, I expect. What do you think I am? I want somebody with a mind.'

'But he doesn't do it with his mind. You're not being logical, my dear.'

I said it and I wondered if I was right. The trouble was that, as with many women, Finnula's genitalia were in her brain, somewhere in the region of the pineal gland.

She couldn't wait any longer to lose her pearl. For days she wore a hardened now-or-never look on her face. She stopped studying and sat in the College library staring into space with a book open in front of her. She took long baths, steeping her body in the oils of rosemary, pine and honeysuckle as if to lave her very entrails. Then she phoned her Moral Tutor. He was busy correcting examination scripts. But she called on him anyway with a punnet of fresh strawberries and a bottle of Bailey's Irish Cream. Then and there, as she bent to wash the strawberries in the wash hand-basin, he raped her.

She claimed he did it in three minutes flat without as much as a kiss or a cuddle.

'What are you doing?' she asked him again and again.

'I'm shoving my cock in your cunt,' he replied like a true British empiricist.

He could not relinquish the habit of logical and cogent thinking even in this problematic situation.

'He took me like a heifer!' snivelled Finnula. 'And then went back to his bloody exam scripts.'

She was sitting on my floor again beside the divan which was her special misery zone. She wore a skimpy beige dress, green stockings and emerald earrings. For a woman who had been raped fifteen minutes earlier she looked very virginal with her bent head and her long hair sluicing down into her lap. To me she looked only half deflowered.

'How could he do it to me?'

'If he did it, it means that he could.' I was only a little sorry for her. 'The question is more how could you have let him?'

'What do you mean?'

'I won't say anything but I won't be silent either. I understand that you wanted to be relieved of your virginity and that is fine with me. What I don't understand is why on earth you chose an Englishman to do it. Can't you see that the whole thing is ideologically repugnant?'

'You just don't seem to understand. For me he is not an Englishman at all. He is a civilized, brilliant – '

I couldn't take it any more. I switched on Radio Free Europe, told her to grow up and go to bed with herself.

The following day a parcel arrived for Finnula. It was from her Moral Tutor. She opened it with trembling hands and a half expectant, half triumphant smile on her face. It died quickly. The package contained a green, white and gold garter belt and a pair of lace panties covered with shamrocks.

I was right after all. In the end it was pure ideology.

After defending my thesis on the Patrimonial Pendulum I went back to Poland and forgot all about Oxford, the easy life and the English disease. Then, one day, I received a postcard from Heidelberg with the picture of a statue of some Greek god or other from the classical museum. The statue was more or less intact except that the penis had fallen off. The postcard read: 'Free at last. Staying in Heidelberg with Prof. Bloomenthal (*the* Bloomenthal). He's Jewish, brilliant and tender. What should I do? F.'

I remembered Bloomenthal. He had been a visiting fellow at the College. He was tall, grey as a pigeon, and seventy-two years old.

I was very pleased that Finnula had written her address in full. People often omit it from postcards. I wrote back a registered, express letter to make sure that it got out of Poland.

Dear Finnula,

Great to hear from you. Forgive my importunity but I've run short of some basics since coming back. I wonder if you could send me the following:

(1) Package of Colombian coffee
(2) Bayer aspirin
(3) Raisins
(4) Vegetable stock
(5) Tampons (large)
(6) Tights (jasmine)
(7) Package of Dunhills

(8) Swiss army knife
(9) Carton of matches
(10)Lancôme night cream (only if on sale)

Please send the package to my University address and mark it 'Books'.

Biodh rud agat féin, nó bí ina éamuis.

FOR THE BEST IN PAPERBACKS, LOOK FOR THE

In every corner of the world, on every subject under the sun, Penguin represents quality and variety—the very best in publishing today.

For complete information about books available from Penguin—including Pelicans, Puffins, Peregrines, and Penguin Classics—and how to order them, write to us at the appropriate address below. Please note that for copyright reasons the selection of books varies from country to country.

In the United Kingdom: For a complete list of books available from Penguin in the U.K., please write to *Dept E.P., Penguin Books Ltd, Harmondsworth, Middlesex, UB7 0DA.*

In the United States: For a complete list of books available from Penguin in the U.S., please write to *Dept BA, Penguin*, Box 120, Bergenfield, New Jersey 07621-0120.

In Canada: For a complete list of books available from Penguin in Canada, please write to *Penguin Books Canada Ltd, 10 Alcorn Avenue, Suite 300, Toronto, Ontario, Canada M4V 3B2.*

In Australia: For a complete list of books available from Penguin in Australia, please write to the *Marketing Department, Penguin Books Ltd, P.O. Box 257, Ringwood, Victoria 3134.*

In New Zealand: For a complete list of books available from Penguin in New Zealand, please write to the *Marketing Department, Penguin Books (NZ) Ltd, Private Bag, Takapuna, Auckland 9.*

In India: For a complete list of books available from Penguin, please write to *Penguin Overseas Ltd, 706 Eros Apartments, 56 Nehru Place, New Delhi, 110019.*

In Holland: For a complete list of books available from Penguin in Holland, please write to *Penguin Books Nederland B.V., Postbus 195, NL-1380AD Weesp, Netherlands.*

In Germany: For a complete list of books available from Penguin, please write to *Penguin Books Ltd, Friedrichstrasse 10-12, D-6000 Frankfurt Main 1, Federal Republic of Germany.*

In Spain: For a complete list of books available from Penguin in Spain, please write to *Longman, Penguin España, Calle San Nicolas 15, E-28013 Madrid, Spain.*

In Japan: For a complete list of books available from Penguin in Japan, please write to *Longman Penguin Japan Co Ltd, Yamaguchi Building, 2-12-9 Kanda Jimbocho, Chiyoda-Ku, Tokyo 101, Japan.*

FOR THE BEST LITERATURE, LOOK FOR THE

☐ **THE BOOK AND THE BROTHERHOOD**
Iris Murdoch

Many years ago Gerard Hernshaw and his friends banded together to finance a political and philosophical book by a monomaniacal Marxist genius. Now opinions have changed, and support for the book comes at the price of moral indignation; the resulting disagreements lead to passion, hatred, a duel, murder, and a suicide pact. *602 pages   ISBN: 0-14-010470-4*

☐ **GRAVITY'S RAINBOW**
Thomas Pynchon

Thomas Pynchon's classic antihero is Tyrone Slothrop, an American lieutenant in London whose body anticipates German rocket launchings. Surely one of the most important works of fiction produced in the twentieth century, *Gravity's Rainbow* is a complex and awesome novel in the great tradition of James Joyce's *Ulysses*. *768 pages   ISBN: 0-14-010661-8*

☐ **FIFTH BUSINESS**
Robertson Davies

The first novel in the celebrated "Deptford Trilogy," which also includes *The Manticore* and *World of Wonders*, *Fifth Business* stands alone as the story of a rational man who discovers that the marvelous is only another aspect of the real. *266 pages   ISBN: 0-14-004387-X*

☐ **WHITE NOISE**
Don DeLillo

Jack Gladney, a professor of Hitler Studies in Middle America, and his fourth wife, Babette, navigate the usual rocky passages of family life in the television age. Then, their lives are threatened by an "airborne toxic event"—a more urgent and menacing version of the "white noise" of transmissions that typically engulfs them. *326 pages   ISBN: 0-14-007702-2*

FOR THE BEST LITERATURE, LOOK FOR THE

□ **A SPORT OF NATURE**
Nadine Gordimer

Hillela, Nadine Gordimer's "sport of nature," is seductive and intuitively gifted at life. Casting herself adrift from her family at seventeen, she lives among political exiles on an East African beach, marries a black revolutionary, and ultimately plays a heroic role in the overthrow of apartheid.

354 pages   ISBN: 0-14-008470-3

□ **THE COUNTERLIFE**
Philip Roth

By far Philip Roth's most radical work of fiction, *The Counterlife* is a book of conflicting perspectives and points of view about people living out dreams of renewal and escape. Illuminating these lives is the skeptical, enveloping intelligence of the novelist Nathan Zuckerman, who calculates the price and examines the results of his characters' struggles for a change of personal fortune.

372 pages   ISBN: 0-14-009769-4

□ **THE MONKEY'S WRENCH**
Primo Levi

Through the mesmerizing tales told by two characters—one, a construction worker/philosopher who has built towers and bridges in India and Alaska; the other, a writer/chemist, rigger of words and molecules—Primo Levi celebrates the joys of work and the art of storytelling.

174 pages   ISBN: 0-14-010357-0

□ **IRONWEED**
William Kennedy

"Riding up the winding road of Saint Agnes Cemetery in the back of the rattling old truck, Francis Phelan became aware that the dead, even more than the living, settled down in neighborhoods." So begins William Kennedy's Pulitzer-Prize winning novel about an ex-ballplayer, part-time gravedigger, and full-time drunk, whose return to the haunts of his youth arouses the ghosts of his past and present.

228 pages   ISBN: 0-14-007020-6

□ **THE COMEDIANS**
Graham Greene

Set in Haiti under Duvalier's dictatorship, *The Comedians* is a story about the committed and the uncommitted. Actors with no control over their destiny, they play their parts in the foreground; experience love affairs rather than love; have enthusiasms but not faith; and if they die, they die like Mr. Jones, by accident.

288 pages   ISBN: 0-14-002766-1

FOR THE BEST LITERATURE, LOOK FOR THE 🐧

☐ **HERZOG**
Saul Bellow

Winner of the National Book Award, *Herzog* is the imaginative and critically acclaimed story of Moses Herzog: joker, moaner, cuckhold, charmer, and truly an Everyman for our time.

342 pages   ISBN: 0-14-007270-5

☐ **FOOLS OF FORTUNE**
William Trevor

The deeply affecting story of two cousins—one English, one Irish—brought together and then torn apart by the tide of Anglo-Irish hatred, *Fools of Fortune* presents a profound symbol of the tragic entanglements of England and Ireland in this century.   *240 pages   ISBN: 0-14-006982-8*

☐ **THE SONGLINES**
Bruce Chatwin

Venturing into the desolate land of Outback Australia—along timeless paths, and among fortune hunters, redneck Australians, racist policemen, and mysterious Aboriginal holy men—Bruce Chatwin discovers a wondrous vision of man's place in the world.   *296 pages   ISBN: 0-14-009429-6*

☐ **THE GUIDE: A NOVEL**
R. K. Narayan

Raju was once India's most corrupt tourist guide; now, after a peasant mistakes him for a holy man, he gradually begins to play the part. His success so well that God himself intervenes to put Raju's new holiness to the test.

220 pages   ISBN: 0-14-009657-4

FOR THE BEST LITERATURE, LOOK FOR THE

☐ **THE LAST SONG OF MANUEL SENDERO**
Ariel Dorfman

In an unnamed country, in a time that might be now, the son of Manuel Sendero refuses to be born, beginning a revolution where generations of the future wait for a world without victims or oppressors.

464 pages ISBN: 0-14-008896-2

☐ **THE BOOK OF LAUGHTER AND FORGETTING**
Milan Kundera

In this collection of stories and sketches, Kundera addresses themes including sex and love, poetry and music, sadness and the power of laughter. "*The Book of Laughter and Forgetting* calls itself a novel," writes John Leonard of *The New York Times*, "although it is part fairly tale, part literary criticism, part political tract, part musicology, part autobiography. It can call itself whatever it wants to, because the whole is genius."

240 pages ISBN: 0-14-009693-0

☐ **TIRRA LIRRA BY THE RIVER**
Jessica Anderson

Winner of the Miles Franklin Award, Australia's most prestigious literary prize, *Tirra Lirra by the River* is the story of a woman's seventy-year search for the place where she truly belongs. Nora Porteous's series of escapes takes her from a small Australia town to the suburbs of Sydney to London, where she seems finally to become the woman she always wanted to be.

142 pages ISBN: 0-14-006945-3

☐ **LOVE UNKNOWN**
A. N. Wilson

In their sweetly wild youth, Monica, Belinda, and Richeldis shared a bachelor-girl flat and became friends for life. Now, twenty years later, A. N. Wilson charts the intersecting lives of the three women through the perilous waters of love, marriage, and adultery in this wry and moving modern comedy of manners.

202 pages ISBN: 0-14-010190-X

☐ **THE WELL**
Elizabeth Jolley

Against the stark beauty of the Australian farmlands, Elizabeth Jolley portrays an eccentric, affectionate relationship between the two women—Hester, a lonely spinster, and Katherine, a young orphan. Their pleasant, satisfyingly simple life is nearly perfect until a dark stranger invades their world in a most horrifying way.

176 pages ISBN: 0-14-008901-2